Children of the Moon

To Jennie.

Reach for the

CHILDREN of the MOON

•

ANTHONY DeSA

Doubleday Canada

Doubleday Canada and colophon are registered trademarks of Penguin Random House Canada Limited.

Library and Archives Canada Cataloguing in Publication

De Sa, Anthony, author
Children of the moon / Anthony De Sa.

Issued in print and electronic formats.
ISBN 978-0-385-68597-9 (hardcover). —ISBN 978-0-385-68598-6 (EPUB)

I. Title.

PS8607.E7515C45 2019   C813'.6   C2018-906038-7
                                               C2018-906039-5

Canada Council   Conseil des arts
for the Arts   du Canada

ONTARIO ARTS COUNCIL
CONSEIL DES ARTS DE L'ONTARIO
an Ontario government agency
un organisme du gouvernement de l'Ontario

TORONTO   FUNDED BY
ARTS   THE CITY OF
COUNCIL   TORONTO

Jacket and book design by Terri Nimmo
Jacket image: Kseniya Zvereva / Getty Images

Printed and bound in the USA

Published in Canada by Doubleday Canada,
a division of Penguin Random House Canada Limited

www.penguinrandomhouse.ca

10 9 8 7 6 5 4 3 2 1

Penguin
Random House
DOUBLEDAY CANADA

For Stephanie

✳

No longer forward nor behind
    I look in hope or fear;
But, grateful, take the good I find,
    The best of now and here.

JOHN GREENLEAF WHITTIER, "My Psalm"

1.

A Beautiful Power

Pó

STANDING IN THE SHADOW of my balcony, I look beyond the hotel grounds to where the brown mouth of the Buzi River meets the Beira harbour, then out, out towards the open sea.

"I was born near the mountain of two peaks. White men called it Kilimanjaro."

Serafim sits in a chair in my room and listens to my words. He is a journalist from Brazil, sent here, to Beira, to record my story for *National Geographic*. I know very little about him, except that I am comforted by the scritch-scratch of his pencil on paper and the crinkles around his eyes.

"My people, the Maasai, have always called that place Oldoinyo Oibor—White Mountain. They say the snowy peak, Kibo, is the house where all gods live."

"Do you believe in God?" Serafim asks.

"There are no gods left. They have been driven off the mountain. If they ever were there."

I turn slightly because I am curious to see his reaction. His face is down, looking at his hand move his pencil over paper. He is fifty—a solid man, his body strong and straight, his once-compact frame still visible under a layer of fat. His hair, the colour of warm sand, is parted on the side. Grease tames it into waves. His brown eyes are set close together and float above his small nose, made smaller by his bushy moustache. He needs a shave.

Serafim adjusts himself on the chair, the same chair he has been sitting on during this past week, ever since he arrived. He sat patiently, interviewing those I had invited to speak to him. They were mostly women and children, the men unwilling to trust an outsider and reluctant to share their stories of fear with another man.

Serafim clears his throat. He pinches the cigarette that rests in the ashtray and draws in the smoke. It comes out his nose in two streams that slow, then curl together.

"Is that why you are here? Looking for gods?" It is too late to soften the edges of my words, but I know he does not care whether I believe in God. That's not why he's here.

In the past, journalists like Serafim had travelled great distances to meet me. They talked of the bigger world and how it was hungry to hear of my work. They brought food and school supplies for the children, and so I welcomed them. They promised my story would help end the threat faced by people like me. Their letters were thin and tilted forward as if they were being pushed from behind. I call them scribblers, because I once allowed myself to love a man who scribbled down his thoughts.

"I've startled you," Serafim says, packing his things. "I guess today's interview didn't get off to a very good start." I hear his satchel snap shut.

I adjust my eyeglasses. When I turn around, to lean against the balcony railing, Serafim is already standing near the door, his bag slung across one shoulder and pressed flat against his thigh. He moves to drop his cigarette in the hallway, but catches himself, and instead bends down to douse it in a small puddle by the wall. His hands are always clean. His nails trimmed. He tucks the cigarette butt into his pocket. *This man cares about the world.*

"I can come back tomorrow. Or Sunday, if you like. When you have more time. If you'll allow me, that is."

I catch his scent—warm clove and curing tobacco. I close my eyes and my toes clench. I loosen my shawl. "Let me speak."

"Please," Serafim says, and there is such urgency in his voice that I want to weep.

"There is nothing worse in this world than to be silenced," I say, and Serafim's body relaxes against the door jamb. "Except, perhaps, being forgotten."

Other journalists have come before him looking for facts. I have given them what they have asked, only to never hear from them again. I was left feeling used and empty. No more. I am grateful I have hunted down words over the years so that I can begin to construct a story—a story that is my own.

"People tell me I was born in 1956, or close to it. I do not disagree, but it means nothing to me. This is what I know. I grew up on the grasslands of Tanganyika, before the land became Tanzania. My people did not care about Europeans or the names they gave things. They drew lines wherever they wanted and claimed what wasn't theirs. The Maasai are a proud people. We kept ourselves alive. The foreigners had all heard our story."

"Story?"

"How the God, Enkai, sent the cattle to our people down a long rope between heaven and earth."

The ocean breeze blows through my window, a distant smell of the salty monsoon sea and charcoal fires.

"We had been given everything. Until one of us tried to demand more from Enkai. He got angry and cut that rope. But you don't need to know all this."

"Please, continue. I want to hear it."

Over and over I have rehearsed how I would tell this story. But this is the first time I have heard my words. I have to push past my uncertainty. "We were sent out of the garden, climbed up from a crater bounded on all sides by a steep cliff. The red dust clung to our skin. We survived the sun and dry lands for countless moons, herding our beasts along the great river they call Nile, walking by the rim of Enkai's angry gash in the earth they also named, Great Rift Valley. You see, the white man has always wanted to tell our story—to name things. The Maasai had nothing they could take. They feared us as warriors—they could not possess us and sell us to foreign lands. And for these reasons they left us alone."

I look over my balcony once again, out across the hotel grounds. Small fires are everywhere. A man has caught some pigeons and is plucking them. Some children are bathing in the stagnant water that has collected in the deep end of the pool. They do so under the bright red light that pulsates from the Coca-Cola machine. It was delivered to that spot, set up against what once was the cabana wall, shortly after the Africa Cup of Nations in 2013. They ran wires to connect that one machine. I have never seen anyone buy anything from it. It accepts nothing but South African rand. This building I live in was once called the Grande Hotel, but its rich guests haven't walked these ruined halls for years. In 1974 the Portuguese soldiers who fought the last days of the War of Independence returned to Portugal and the hotel was left in ruins. As soon as we had taken back our land we entered a war amongst ourselves. Another twenty years of bloodshed, but those soldiers had no need for the hotel. It is now home to over two thousand people. There is no running water and no electricity. The city's politicians leave us alone. They know if you poke a stick into an anthill, the ants scurry about, clean up the mess and strengthen things, as if erasing the action. With its many ghosts we share the hotel and drink leaking rainwater. Elevator shafts have become dark throats that swallow our waste, and at least once a year a child falls in and is lost to us. The war has scarred this place. Serafim can see that for himself.

"Here we are all broken—the lame, the poor, refugees, and albinos like me. We each have found a place. People with albinism have taken over Block B of the hotel. Here in Mozambique we are misunderstood. We are attacked, killed. Our body parts are sold to men who call themselves healers for use in charms and magical potions. But you have heard this."

"Do you ever think of going back to the place you were born? Would you be safe there?" From the strength of his voice I know he has returned to the chair I set out for him.

"We are called *zeru zerus* there. It means we are nothing. Here, the people call me a *branca*. Albinos who do not belong to others have come here because they have heard of this place, and of me. I have no special magic, but I cannot convince them."

Lulled by the sound of Serafim scratching his notes, I continue. What comes through the gate of my mouth is carefully selected.

"If there *is* a god, the one my ancestors called Enkai, I have seen its face in three women. These were the strong ones who never feared my touch. Namunyak, my birth mother, gave me life and a name. She would not live long enough to see me laugh or play or take my first steps. Simu, my mother's sister, took me in and nurtured a place of love in me so that I would not grow into a bitter root. Fatima, the last of the three women, she christened me Pó, the Portuguese word for powder. 'A fitting name for a beautiful girl like you,' she said."

Serafim looks up from his notebook. His face glows.

"I have also seen the face of god in one man," I say. "Ezequiel. He kept a harmonica in his pocket, an extra pair of boots over his shoulder, and a rifle across his back. He declared his love for me with a gift. And later he gave me another." I catch my breath. "Because of Zeca, I can see things as Enkai had intended." I remember thinking, *This is the way the world is. This is the way the world was meant to be.*

Serafim

I UNDO MY BELT and pour myself a Scotch. I should call reception to collect my laundry. It all needs to be washed for tomorrow. Everything I possess can fit in one bag. Travelling light and owning little has always given me the freedom to pick up and leave.

I kick off my shoes and press the heels of my bare feet against the balcony's railing. The last story I wrote was for a national magazine—"Untouched by Civilization: The Hidden Peoples of the Amazon." I spent months in a remote part of the Brazilian jungle getting closer to what I was certain was a previously unidentified tribe. The story and photos went viral. Anthropologists were horrified that I had dared to chronicle these people they had never heard about. They wanted answers, coordinates, confirmation. I needed to get away, take some time and consider how to live with what I had done—bringing these untouched tribes to a hungry world that couldn't get enough. I got too close, exposed them to disease, and opened unprotected lands to illegal gold mining. All for the story.

I take off my shirt, knot one of the sleeves to the balcony railing. I light a cigarette, top off my drink, and take a swig, feel the burn.

Shortly after I checked into the Hotel Tivoli, I dragged a chair and table out onto the fourth-floor balcony of my corner room, arranging them so that I could see bits of the ocean to my left and the fragile buildings of this poor city to my right. The shouts from shop vendors and street brawls that spilled from bars onto dirt roads, the smell of smoke from outdoor kitchen fires, all reminded me of the favela where I was raised. Like Serrinha and surrounding Florianópolis, there's nothing beautiful about this city; nothing about its architecture inspires me, except at dusk when lights twinkle from apartments or the glow from open storefronts floods the streets, and I think of quieter times.

The first week with Pó was filled with her graphic accounts of the many who had come to the Grande Hotel to see her, to share their stories of survival. Interviews with PWAs—persons with albinism—were granted. Pó was always in the room to interpret my questions, to offer short bursts of detail to clarify stories of fear and torture. When I interviewed Winfrida Mbiti, it was Pó who recounted her story. The young woman sat in her chair, her face turned to the side; she would not look at me. Winfrida had been lured away by an uncle and cousin. They took her into the bush to help them look for stray goats. There they hacked at her arm. Her ear had been cut off. Much later, during a church service, her cousin broke down and told the pastor everything: his role, how he held her down as his father mutilated her. They were both sent to trial, but were set free. When Winfrida healed, she ran away. When I asked Pó why Winfrida would not look at me, did I frighten her, Pó said that the only way she could hear me was by turning her good ear toward me.

Pó provided me with the names of people who had been attacked, murdered, and even those whose graves had been robbed. But it is the unwillingness of the police or government authorities to address the atrocities that takes so much out of her. The fight is draining her and she looks frail. I am committed to reporting her story as she tells it. I have been detached, an observer who keeps one eye open and the other eye, the passionate eye, shut.

No more. From now on, both eyes wide open.

The small recorder rests next to my drink. I take another sip and light another cigarette. The smoke curls up toward the half-lit sky. I conjure Pó in my mind—her long frame standing on the balcony, the curve of her back turned to me, her shuka clinging to her body. I let the shape of her take form. I press Play.

❋

"When did you realize you were—"

"Different?"

"Yes."

"If I think hard and close my eyes until there is only darkness, I can hear my mother's heartbeat still. You may not believe me when I say I can remember the smell of my birth, of dried grass and earth and smoke and the sticky stench of blood."

"Are you sure you do remember? Might it be that these details were told to you by Simu or others in the village?"

"You don't believe me?"

"I'm sorry. Please continue."

"I was not meant to survive. I was born in my mother's hut. My aunt Simu recalled how that night the roof leaked with the drip-drip of rain. She looked after my mother, soothing her with stories that the raindrops were tears of joy from the gods to greet me. My father saw it differently. He stayed nearby, with the other men, waiting. The rain under a fat moon was the sign he had been looking for. He would have a strong son, worthy of a great warrior. My mother pushed me out into a warm evening, where I took my first breath. I was told this story countless times by Simu. I never tired of it. The moment I slipped out from my mother I was greeted by the moonlight that crept into the mouth of our mud hut. My pale body dragged across my mother's belly and to her breast. My skin, white as bone. A curse. A moon child, the men muttered, before running away. Simu remained to soothe the concern in her sister's eyes.

"I did not cry, but my hungry breaths took up too much air. Simu poured some milk between my mother's lips, and my mother spat it on the ground. She then pinched milk from her own breast and sprinkled it on the ground as well—a gift for Olapa, goddess of the moon and wife to Enkai, god of the sun. Simu would often recount the story of how Olapa had once wounded Enkai. To cover up his wound, he took to shining so bright that no one could look straight at him and see his shame. To punish Olapa, Enkai plucked out one of her eyes. You can still see her missing eye."

"And your father's reaction?"

"My father thrust himself into the entrance. Simu pressed her back to the mud wall. She said he was a handsome man of graceful bearing. That night, when he saw me feeding, he turned ugly. He reached down for me with one hand and with his other hand raised his warrior sticks.

"'You know we must rid ourselves of this curse,' he said.

"'This is your child,' my mother told him. 'If you do not claim her then she will be mine—mine to me. She will not be killed. She will live to walk and be free.'"

"He relented."

"My father knew she would fight to the death. He backed out of the hut and tore at the marriage necklace my mother had made for him. Blue-black beads showered down on us. Villagers had called on Tonkei, our oloiboni, who arrived before the sun."

"I'm sorry, what's an oloiboni?"

"Our healer. A dried twig of a man, he wrapped himself in a lion's hide and wore a headdress of ostrich feathers that made him appear bigger and more powerful than he was. Simu did not want him there, but word had spread. Tonkei said he was a descendant of Enkai made in two forms—the black god, who was benevolent, and the red god, who was vengeful. Simu saw only the red god in Tonkei, all cunning and mischief. He told prophecies to collect money or food, sold amulets and necklaces in exchange for his protection or potions. When displeased or angered, he cursed the rains to stay away or he ordered the cows' udders to dry and crack.

"Early that morning, Tonkei called up to the gods. He shook stones from a gourd, looked at how they had fallen. The answer was clear to him. The gods would decide my fate. It was no sign. For hundreds of years milk-skinned children like me had faced the same test.

"Tonkei crept into the hut while my mother slept and took me from her. 'It is the colour of a dead tooth,' he said.

"Upon hearing his words, my mother shook herself clear of the hides and shukas that entangled her legs, dragged herself with what little strength she had to the opening of our hut. People had gathered around the fire. Brightness washed over them under a hunter's moon. My father stood in the distance. Tonkei placed me naked on the ground, and I squirmed in front of the thorn-brush kraal. Simu remembered the rain pouring down, but I did not cry. The latch was unhinged and the gate flung wide. The herd pounded their shadows until the earth stopped trembling and the world grew quiet once again.

"The villagers were content that Enkai had made a wise decision. My mother sobbed into her hands. My father's howl faded behind the trail of cattle dust. In that moment, the instant when the moon gives way to the break of dawn, the shrill cry of a newborn pierced the stillness."

"It is a remarkable story."

"You don't believe it?"

"Do you?"

Ezequiel

"I'M NOT AFRAID, you know." My words chase the home-care nurse as she closes the door behind her.

I have always kept quiet and to myself. Even when I worked, I'd hurry home to my basement apartment, careful that no one followed. But it isn't fear.

The two basement windows are rotting from years of rain and cold. One of the nurses, Helen, I think it was, told me that the windows are not up to code—too small, she said. They do let in the harsh light of a motion detector the neighbour installed between our houses. A cat or raccoon triggers it repeatedly. The floors are painted concrete and the whole place smells like soggy bread.

I like to keep the radio on all day. The music reminds me of Papa Gilberto's windup record player. It had its own spot underneath his office window. A bookcase took up most of the wall. Papa's collection of records and his books were arranged by subject: history, government, religion, but also books of poetry and novels, all organized neatly on the shelf. From his office window, I could look out onto cloud shadows creeping over the plains of high grass, over the thorn trees and the occasional outcrop of rock out to a horizon of purple hills, dotted with acacia, sycamore, fig, and mimosa trees, and the two baobabs at opposite corners of our land. A ribbon of forest ran along the river that cut into our mission. I can never return.

My kitchen window, above the sink and the tiled backsplash, is rectangular and faces the neighbour's wall. From my La-Z-Boy I can see brick, a triangle of sky, and some green from a maple tree. When the neighbour walks between our houses I can see his knees and up his shorts. He has told me his name, but I can't remember it. The refrigerator whistles for five minutes every time I open the door, and on the freezer door a magnet of the Canadian flag holds a hockey calendar, its squares empty. During the cold months, the boiler rages then hums behind the plantation doors I installed to hide the guts of the house, the boiler and the hot water tank and copper pipes like intestines. When the repairman is called in, I show him the doors and lock myself in my bedroom. At the end of a short corridor is a fire door, which leads to twelve steps rising to the backyard. On good days, I garden.

I bought the house years ago, but it was too big for me. I moved into the basement and I've had the same tenants renting out the top floors for the last fifteen years. I haven't raised their rent since they moved in.

I hardly go out anymore. I stopped working—I was a night custodian—two years ago, when things got bad, when the doctor diagnosed Lewy body dementia, basically a cocktail of Alzheimer's and Parkinson's disease. Sixty-four is a bit young to show signs of degenerative disease, the doctors say, even though I tell them my memory is stronger than ever. They asked if I had any questions but they didn't answer them. Why are my veins turning into electric wires? How come my dreams are flooded with colour? Why do imposters chase me every night? The Commander is after me. I tried to convince them he has connections that reach far beyond Mozambique.

My brain tires. All my senses have dulled to the outside world. I don't deserve to participate in life, not after what I saw and what I did. I used to catch myself smiling—children playing, piri piri shrimp, *All in the Family*—and I would feel guilty for letting joy creep inside me. They give me risperidone, which dulls the noises in my head and lets me drift off to a time and place where everything seems real. I keep telling myself that it's better not to look back. Nothing good comes from going back. Now, I spend part of my day or what is left of the night in my bed or in my chair staring into the dark until my eyes can pierce the thickness to see clearly through it. I see people, animals, and objects all around me, though they try to hide in the carpet pattern or in the paintings on the wall. I never switch lights on in the basement. I like it this way.

"I used to have a dream as a boy—not a nightmare," I say. Then I realize I am alone. Still, I'm careful not to speak too loudly or to give too much away. You never know who is listening.

Once I could fly. Well, it wasn't flying, exactly—more like jumping from treetop to treetop, high above the ground. When I looked down, a crowd of people gazed up; they saw me in the canopy bounding from one tree to the next, sometimes tumbling and flipping with an ease that stretched their mouths wide open. As I jumped, I felt flashes of light bursting from my body, so dazzling. They watched from below and shouted, "The wheel! Ezequiel has turned into the wheel!" I looked down and was suddenly fearful. I began to lose my weightlessness. I could feel myself getting heavy, sinking into the leaves and branches that no longer supported me. The crowds, all their anxious faces unknown to me, flashed by me as I crashed through the canopy of trees.

Life is a dizzying second.

I look out my window and enter the jungle and surge toward the backdrop of a world I faintly recognize. I want to go back to when I was a boy. *Papa!* I yell. *Papa!* But before he can turn to face me a blaze of white grabs hold of me and lifts me up to the sky. Mother Anke smiles, tosses me into the air again and catches me in her arms. I nuzzle into her neck and smell soap.

✹

Our prayer house was the first building the guerrillas set ablaze. The fire engulfed the structure, and whipped up by the wind, the flames leapt onto the other buildings, until all of our mission was burning. *Adjoining houses always burn*, Papa Gilberto had often said to me, but I don't think that is what the proverb meant. I cup my ears, trying to replace the sound of men's laughter with my parents' voices. *One foot in front of the other*, I hear Papa Gilberto say, and I do not feel my feet touching the ground. But Mother Anke's words make my brain hum: *Do not enter the jungle. There is fear in the dark forest.* She always lit a candle before going to bed—*a candle chases the shadows.*

With every sound, I bite down hard, grind my teeth. I am thirteen and will not cry. We cut a narrow path through the jungle. Looking back at the mission, I see the golden embers and smoke rise up to mingle with the stars. The mission is turning into an upside-down heaven.

When he entered the mission as the leader of his men, he introduced himself as Macaco. He flashed his teeth—upper gums bracketed with large incisors. The missing row of upper teeth, perhaps four, turned his mouth into a gaping pink hole. I'm not sure what Macaco wanted with me—why he chose to spare my life and bring me with them. The boy, Armando, walks behind me. I wonder if he too was taken from his family. Whenever I stagger or when my knees get soft, Armando nudges my back with the muzzle of his gun.

It is night when Macaco falls back and allows one of the other men to lead. He does not look at me when he inserts himself into the line in front of me. I smell the sourness of his body. I trip and fall.

"Get up!" he says, striking my face with the back of his hand. I feel nothing.

"You will march with us or I will tie a stone to your ankles and throw you in the river."

I get up and straighten my legs. *One step followed by another.* I know I want to live. *One step turns to a hundred then a thousand and then ten thousand.* I hear his voice but can't see Papa Gilberto's face. Every time I try, my thoughts turn black. Mother Anke is always clear—tall, broad-shouldered, with a heavy bosom and hips. Her hands were bigger than Papa's and they were always red, like her cheeks. Her mouth was wide. She kept her cinnamon-coloured hair pulled back tight in a bun, which made her eyes appear squinty—eyes blue like sea ice, she liked to say, even though it did not help me understand. She was uncomfortable in the heat. Her fair skin wasn't suited to the sun, and her clothes were rough and chafed against her.

Mother Anke and Papa Gilberto were not my birth parents. "Your mother was an *entertainer*," Mother Anke once told me, her face twisted as if she had bitten into an overripe mango. "Only three days old and she left you on the kitchen table, like a cut of meat," she said. Over the years I had pieced bits together. I know my father was white and Portuguese, but I do not know his name. From gossip and conversation I overheard between workers, I learned he was a government worker from Lisbon who visited the hotel where my mother had a room and worked. He always chose my mother because she was more beautiful than the other women. I once heard Mother Anke say that many men asked for my mother. She never used her name. Lázaro, my favourite mission worker, shared it with me. *Eugenia*, he whispered once, while he taught me to groom my father's horse.

Where am I? I see the calendar on my refrigerator and my panic eases. I hear a police siren outside. Someone's knocking on the door, the renters arguing on the main floor, the flushing of a toilet, and the slapping sound the neighbour's sandals make against his heels.

Noise.

We move at night, hide and sleep during the day. When the sun rises, Macaco raises his fist in the air and the men drop where they stand. After a few minutes, they begin to stir and make themselves nests of grasses and branches. Takudzwa, who belongs to the Shona tribe, appears with a headless snake draped around his neck. He falls to his knees and scores the snake before pulling the skin back in one long piece. The small morsels of meat fill my belly. Armando climbs the tree trunk, his legs and arms moving together in short bursts until he reaches the first large branch. He looks down at me. Directing with his chin, he points to an empty branch. I'm not as quick as he is, but I get up there and stretch my body out to nestle into the bough. Our heads are a foot apart. I listen to his breathing.

"His name is Malik," Armando whispers in Portuguese, "but you only refer to him as Leader. Never call him Macaco." Unlike the other men, Armando looks at me when he speaks. "The men told me prazeiros gave him that nickname as a boy. He uses the name landowners gave him to feed his rage."

I do not know if it was my African blood that kept me alive or the idea that Macaco could possess the part of me he resented, the same way he held on to the awful name.

Armando tells me he was raised on colonial land. His family cultivated the fields but were given little for their hard work. His father encouraged him to run away—to search for a better life. "My mother used to say there are two places we are always moving toward: where it all ends and where it all began," he whispers, shifting his body to gaze into the canopy of trees. "It's a beautiful place." I close my eyes and slip my hands into my pockets, where I touch the smooth surface of Papa Gilberto's harmonica.

In those first weeks I was drawn to Armando. I learned he was fourteen, a year older than me, and had been with these men for two years. He did not give details about his parents, if they were still alive. I had heard whispers about young men being forced by rebels to kill their families and burn their villages. I never thought they were talking about boys.

As the men slept, I thought of the safest place in the world—Papa's office. It comforted me to imagine the Persian rug covering the floor, the pieces of furniture never moved from their spots. Papa didn't like to move things, and he saw no reason to *fiddle*. He was away often, travelling to estate sales as far as Porto Amélia. He witnessed growing unrest and frustration. Pleas and petitions proved useless. Peaceful protests were met by violence. In June 1960, hundreds of unarmed people in the northern town of Mueda assembled for a peaceful meeting. They were murdered.

Rumblings of war were driving the Portuguese out of Mozambique. Papa Gilberto told me about the Mueda massacre and about a brave man called Eduardo Mondlane, the leader of Frente de Libertação de Moçambique—FRELIMO. They were only fighting for what was theirs.

Many Portuguese families, some who had been in Mozambique for hundreds of years, were leaving everything behind and going to live in Portugal, a place foreign and unfamiliar to them—or at least that's what Papa said. These landowners, prazeiros, were afraid that all would be taken from them, or worse, if they did not leave.

My parents stayed to do God's work. We couldn't call it that or the Portuguese government would close us down, like they had every other Dutch Reformed Church in Mozambique. We called ourselves evangelists, and our mission the Mission of God. Papa's answer was always the same: "God is on our side. We are doing His good work." But one night I overheard Mother Anke and Papa talking. Papa said the Portuguese were fools. Many families, like his, had been in Mozambique for generations, but more Portuguese were arriving daily on its shores. The government was giving them free land, and this was adding fuel to the flame. Papa said you couldn't give away that which was not yours to give. Mother Anke pleaded with him to leave, tried to convince him the mission would never be a home. She reminded him that he had promised her only ten years; that he would take her back home to her parents in Holland when his work was done. Mother Anke never liked Mozambique—she was afraid of the jungle because even the plants had claws. Once she told me, "All things in this country are trained to bite, Zeca. The birds tear at the sky, the branches shred the clouds, and even the earth hisses when the rain falls." In 1964 the Mozambican War of Independence officially began. The same year, I was taken from my family.

Papa Gilberto would say that just as the seeds of a mango tree undergo a change from seeds to tree, getting stronger and more firmly rooted, so too grow the mission and followers of God.

"To die a tribe and be born a nation." A FRELIMO political slogan. I keep repeating it. Not too loud; you can't trust anyone.

In 1965, guerrillas launched attacks on targets in northern

Mozambique. Macaco and his men, including me, were never part of that. We weren't even part of one of those official, small, platoon-sized engagements. We were always far from where the fighting was taking place. We lived in the bush, foraged from the local villages. What they did not offer, we took.

I wake up in a sweat. I want water. I can hear it dripping from the kitchen sink, but my legs do not move. There is nothing but a clock on my nightstand. The numbers glow 2:43. I lay my head back down. When I feel disoriented, the doctors have told me to think of the number three to calm my nerves. Everything comes in threes: Neapolitan ice cream, *The Good, the Bad, and the Ugly*, the red, amber, green of a traffic light, a tricycle . . . the Portuguese army's objectives: to destroy as much of the people's food as possible in an effort to starve them out; to terrorize the people and make them feel unsafe and insecure, instilling the idea that FRELIMO could not help them; to destroy every man, woman, and child who believes in Mondlane's mantra, *A luta continua*—the struggle continues.

I am determined to keep moving. Papa used to say that everyone complains about the sun's scorching heat, the rains that wash away roads, the winds that topple huts, the drought that kills thousands, but there is never bitterness directed at the moon.

His words keep me strong at night, even though my back aches from the weight of supplies and the gun strap cutting across my shoulder blades. I use the muzzle to scratch my forehead. It would be so easy to end things with a quick pull of the trigger. I think about this when I am hungry. It has been only a few weeks since leaving the mission and we have travelled through jungle and over hills. The day's warmth has dwindled and my skin tingles. In my dream I sprint across the treetops as fast as I can, my toes barely touching the leaves. "Go, Zeca! Go far!" I leap, fly. Beads of sweat splash my shoulders and arms. The sun sinks lower but I do not stop. I muster a second wind and keep pushing myself to reach the finish. But the sliver of sun slips away over the hills faster than I can fly. My heart sinks with it as it drops from my sight. The sky turns dark. I wobble on my feet, spent, and then I tumble into the canopy, my limbs getting tangled in the branches that break my fall.

Every so often the sound of running water or the roar of a waterfall draws us away from our path. Macaco tells us how long we can stay, which fruits to eat or roots to boil. I have learned nothing about this leader. I can't imagine what happened in his life to bring him here. All I know is what I see. He carries a radio transmitter on his back. Macaco has us believe we are part of a bigger plan, fighting for the brotherhood. I am not convinced. We have not made contact with other FRELIMO soldiers. Macaco has not received any directives in months. There are no maps, and we wander aimlessly in circles. No one dares ask Macaco why.

———

Climbing out of the jungle's shadow, we reach a tea plantation, the pickers in the distance, half their bodies lost in a green sea of leaves. Farther off, smoke billows from what must be their village. Warmth surges through my body; it reaches the tips of my fingers and my toes. There will be people and families and prayer. I allow myself the hope that Papa Gilberto is alive and may be waiting in the village for me. Mother Anke will be with him and she'll run to me, her rough hands will draw me near.

The rains come down hard and the soil turns to mud. It doesn't take long before my boots sink in deep, releasing the sharp odour of soaked soil. If I drop any deeper I'm afraid I'll disappear. The skin on my feet will pucker and rot. All I think of is the warm fire that will greet us in the centre of the village. There will be food in a large pot and they will welcome us because we are tired and hungry and we are fighting for them.

I shiver, and Armando, by my side, wraps his arms around me to keep me warm. He nods, tells me he understands with his silent smile, and I lean into him. Every so often when he is sleeping, he kicks out in a panic, stabs out a word or two, and it is my turn to calm him.

I mark my days with knots in my bootlaces. Three months on and there is no more room for knotting. I pull thread from the hems of my pants—one strand for each day. Forty knots and eighty-six threads of frayed cotton so far. I am beginning to let go of the world I came from. I cannot reclaim Mother Anke and Papa Gilberto.

"You can never go back," Armando whispers as if reading my thoughts. "Believe me," he says.

The day these men came and walked into the clearing has washed away like the rains erase the track of animals. Another night falls. I will hold my gun to my chest and keep moving.

A dozen or so huts are scattered in the village. No villagers welcome us with food and drink. I see a prayer house next to a kraal. I shiver as a light wind shakes the thatched roofs. I cannot see any footprints and there are no livestock. The birds and the crickets have gone silent. I can hear my heart beating. My body tingles, every part of me alert. Behind me I sense danger, but I refuse to look back. Figures dash from behind a hut into the jungle. Macaco is the first to raise his gun and shoot. All the other men in our group scan the horizon and shoot blindly into the trees. Since being on the march I have yet to shoot. I raise my gun; my hands tremble. The shaking is coming from my insides.

Macaco lifts his hand in the air. The men stop firing, but they do not lower their guns until the forest has grown quiet.

"Why do you hide? You must help us in the fight!" Macaco yells out.

I hear the low call of a woman's voice: "Zabere. Zabere." She rises from the bush near the trees. She has been shot in the leg. She leans against a tree and holds out her hand in Macaco's direction. A frightened young girl, ten or eleven years old, appears. She looks at Macaco as if to ask permission to go to her mother. "Zabere!" The cry is shrill and urgent. The girl takes a few steps. Macaco catches her around the waist. She kicks, tries to reach back and grab hold of Macaco's head or bandolier. His dirty hand muffles her screams. The woman limps out from the edge of the jungle.

"Shoot her," Macaco says to me, spit spraying from his mouth. "You are a soldier now. Shoot!"

The woman looks straight at me, holds out her hands. Her eyes are large and white. "Give me my daughter."

"Shoot her!" Macaco yells. "Or I'll kill them both!"

The words ring in my ears, and I am taken back to my home at the mission, back to the clearing by the well and the old acacia tree. I glance at the girl struggling against Macaco's hip. I raise my rifle to my shoulder to look through the rear sight. I aim. My arm burns with the weight of the gun. My finger feels for the trigger. The woman staggers, places one foot in front of the other before catching a branch to steady herself. I am only now aware that I am sobbing.

"Shoot!"

My fingertip touches the curve of the trigger.

"Shoot! SHOOT!"

I open my eyes and through the smoke's haze the woman stands still, a bullet hole through her neck. There is so much blood.

Zabere's mouth will not close. Out of it comes a silent cry. Macaco suddenly drops her. He presses the sides of his head until his hands tremble. He disappears into the hut, and the girl scrambles to her feet and goes to her mother.

I let my gun fall to the ground. The flesh of my palms and fingertips tingle. I remain on my spot in the clearing, the village around me going up in flames and smoke. The prayer house burns bright. The other men begin to sack the huts—stealing what little money they can find, clothes, food, radios, any other supplies they think might be useful, including rope and wire. Then they light the thatched roofs. The world is blurred by the smoke and embers that float and swirl in the air.

Pó

A FEW WEEKS BEFORE Serafim's arrival, I had stopped getting up in the morning to greet the sun. I spent those hours rubbing the aches from my bones, closing my eyes to push back at the searing pain from open sores across my shoulders and neck. But Serafim's visits have sent a charge of electricity coursing through my veins.

Serafim opens his bag before sitting in his chair. I am happy to share with him today's story, but I have only ever shared it with Amalia and I know I must recount the story in a very different way for him. All night I was anxious about sharing this part of my life. I kept playing it over in my head, trying to manage my recollections in a way that he would understand. He is a sensitive man and he will have questions. Serafim tucks a pencil above his ear and lights a cigarette. He leans forward. I take it as his eagerness to hear my first words.

"I think I was eleven when the river overflowed, its thick brown waters drowning the bushes and vines that grew along its bank. I loved the river. I removed the big hat Simu made me wear under the sun, the shuka that covered my arms. I wiggled my toes in the rusty water and dug my feet into the mud.

"I turned around to see if Lebo stood where I'd told him. I could see his shape, standing with my hat on top of his head, balancing on one foot, holding his spear as if tending the cattle. He was eight. His head was big, the elbows and knees like knots on a stick. When he smiled, and if I was close enough, I could see the gap between his front teeth. I would warn him to keep his mouth closed, not to giggle too much, or else lizards would enter between the gap and make a home. He liked the idea of it.

"'Do not move!' I yelled to him, before closing my eyes and slipping into the river.

"My head went under and a thousand thorns pricked at my skin. I broke the surface and floated on my back. No one taught me to swim. I learned by doing. Lebo's name meant 'born in the bush.' He was my cousin, but Simu said that I was to treat him as my brother. The other children my age did not speak to me. Their parents told them that if they looked me in the eyes they would turn to dust that I would then smear over my face and body to make myself stronger."

"Did everyone believe this? Or did your aunt have any success dispelling the myth?"

"She tried. And I had Lebo. Other than Simu, he was the only other person I loved, or who loved me more. He was gentle, but he was a Maasai, and he would have to learn.

"Simu, whose name meant 'the gentle one,' told me she would never lie to me—that knowing things would give me my voice. She did not want me to grow angry. She told me bitterness would eat away at me like a death worm. Majuto, her husband, was angry when she brought me to live with them. He said I was a curse. Simu told him Enkai had decided I should live and that I was special. 'I will raise my sister's child as my own,' she told Majuto, but he reminded her that she already had a child to look after. Koinet, my cousin, was older and more serious than me, and acted like he was much smarter too. But Simu persisted. The curse would be upon us if she left me to be eaten by animals. And Majuto listened.

"When Koinet had seen fourteen long rains, he told me he was a warrior and I must do things for him or he would punish me.

"'You are a boy,' I said.

"'You are not my sister. You are nothing but a ghost,' he replied."

Serafim stretches his writing hand. He lifts his eyeglasses over his head, traps his hair in their frames. "Do you mind if I tape the rest of your story?"

I don't answer him; I simply continue. "Coming up for air, I checked on Lebo. I knew I would not be allowed to watch over Lebo much longer. He would be taken away from me. 'Boys must learn to herd cows and goats,' Majuto was always saying. I never called Majuto father.

"My mother died the morning I was born. My father was found soon after. The villagers said the same cattle intended to kill me had trampled him. Simu said something else. She said my father drank 'the soup' and demons visited his brain. He bashed his head with his rungu, his throwing club.

"Lebo had not wanted to come to the river. He wanted to catch chameleons. He would spend hours moving them from one spot to the next—bush to bark to rock—to see them change colour until they disappeared. He would never hurt them. Once, his father saw this and got angry. Majuto held a stone and smashed the lizard. 'A boy must hunt and kill.'"

"And how did Majuto and your tribe define you?" Serafim asks.

"I do not understand," I say, even though I know exactly what he is asking.

"If Lebo was defined by his ability to—"

"They could not name something they did not understand. They were afraid of me."

Surprised by the tone of my voice, I continue my story so that perhaps it will answer this question for Serafim—a question I am certain he already knows the answer to.

"It felt good to let go in the current and float. When done, I sat at the river's edge and looked down. Red-brown mud covered my legs. I rubbed more up my arms, onto my shoulders. I smoothed it over the tops of my feet and covered my chest and belly. I dug deep into the river's edge and brought the sludge up to my face. It was warm and smelled of eggs. I smeared it on my cheeks and forehead, across the bridge of my nose, onto my neck. I dredged two large handfuls and pressed them into my hair. I used my fingers to push the mud deep so that it touched my scalp. I leaned over the river and caught my reflection in the water. My skin was now the right colour.

"I could see that I had travelled some distance from where I had entered the bloated river and where I last saw Lebo running after me.

"'Lebo!' I called. He needed to know that I was safe. I waved so he could see me. 'Lebo?' I screened my eyes so that I could look for him. My heart beat fast. I kept calling his name, first walking then running back up the river's bank. The mud was drying quickly and it stretched tight across my skin. I stopped running and listened. That was when I heard a familiar song. I moved in the sound's direction and my stomach began to untwist. I saw him sitting under the shade of a tree, humming his lullaby, the one blessing song Simu would often sing to us.

I quickened my pace until I reached him and dropped to the ground. 'Lebo, you scared me.' He sat hugging his knees in a nest of tall grass. When he turned to me his eyes got big. He crawled over to me and drew his thumb across my cheek. Then he pressed his finger to his lips and directed me to a large rock by the river's edge. I took a few steps towards the rock and saw the flap of a large ear. An elephant calf lay on its side in the dirt near the river. I took a few more careful steps towards the calf and reached back and pointed at Lebo for him to stay. Growing up in the savannah, there was nothing more frightening than to stand between an elephant calf and its mother. I looked around, searching for signs of a herd. I could see Lebo rocking faster. I was ten steps away from the elephant calf when it rolled from its side and struggled to stand on its feet. The elephant raised its trunk in the air and blew."

Serafim exhales loudly.

"My story does not interest you."

"No. It's not that. It's just that I've heard it said that an elephant will not leave its young's side. They often remain for days or weeks after one of their own has died. I guess what I'm wondering is—"

"If what I am telling you is true."

Serafim shifts in his chair.

"The calf's skin was the colour of angry clouds," I say. "The hair on its tail was almost golden, the same colour as my hair. It struggled, but there was no sign of injury. Something about it drew me closer. I had never touched an elephant before. Its body was covered in fine hair. Its skin was tough, and it surprised me that a spear could pierce it. 'You are lost,' I whispered, looking into its eye.

"Lebo's lullaby grew louder. I mimicked his song. Lebo came and stood next to me. He was brave and touched the elephant's head. I smiled at him. I went to the river's edge and cupped water in my hands. By the time I reached the elephant there was little water left, only muddied hands. I wiped the mud on the elephant's leg and the sound it made told me its skin was soothed. It was there for a mud bath, but the riverbank's steep drop and the swift current must have frightened it. Or perhaps it had slipped into the river upstream and had been carried by the water to this place.

"'Lebo, go fill my hat with mud!' He scampered off to the river's edge and when he hobbled back we turned the hat over onto the elephant's side. I returned for more mud and left Lebo to smooth the muck over the elephant's head. "Abák," he called her, as he spread the sludge over the animal and I swept my shuka across its body. Large patches of clay had flaked off my own skin, but some other parts had only cracked and still clung to me. Lebo laughed and called me hyena.

"Thunder rumbled in the distance. The elephant stood up. Lebo crouched behind me and we looked at the elephant with only half of its side covered in mud. The other half, the part of its body that had been touching the ground, was the deep purple of distant mountains. The elephant blinked from its wet eye. Its eyelashes were as long as my fingers. I nestled my fingers in the creases of its trunk. I felt the quiver of its skin."

"And when you returned to the village?" Serafim says.

"We had come as two but went home as three, with Abák following us. We did not walk on the worn path—the mud there swallowed our feet up to our ankles. We cut through higher ground. The rain pelted us and washed my skin of mud, cooled the fire that was burning underneath. We hadn't collected any olive wood and Simu would be angry. Lebo had gathered a few damp twigs, but they were useless.

"We climbed over the hill, hand in hand. My legs ached from the effort. Lebo let go and pressed his hands to his thighs to keep them from shaking. Both of us looked on in silence, catching our breath. I wasn't quite sure how we would explain it. But I was hopeful Simu would take our elephant in the same way she had me."

"What you're saying is that the elephant followed you back to the village?" Serafim says, shaking his head.

Part of me knew he would be skeptical, and a piece of me wants to stop the interview and send him home. He exhales before raising his hand. He fiddles with some buttons on his digital recorder. He presses a button and I continue with my story.

"On a clear day, when I climbed up the old baobab at the top of the hill, I could only make out the stone shape of the manyatta from that place. That day the rains blurred our village. I did not see the huts from that distance, though I knew there were twenty-seven of them inside the fence. We had far more cattle and goats and chickens than people. Only the cattle had separate pens within our village. All the other animals roamed freely. No lions or hyenas could ever get to us, or our livestock. We were protected by a fence of acacia branches. The angry thorns pointed out to ward off hungry animals.

"As we came down the hill, people emerged and disappeared in a grey space that did not belong to water or land or sky. A group of children, who had been running in the rain, stopped chasing their goats. Shouts were heard, villagers assembled at the main gate.

"'You have brought danger here,' Majuto said. He reached for his son's hand and pulled him tight. The crowd let Simu through. Silver circles of metal dangled from her headband. She was noble, beautiful. Koinet stood by his mother. Lebo tore away from his father's hand and hugged Simu. Tonkei, the village healer, was there as well. He shook his gourd and the stones tumbled out onto earth. Many of the villagers ran back behind the safety of the fence. They understood something that I had forgotten. Abák's small toot was echoed by a much louder reply. A female elephant stood at the top of the ridge. I heard the villagers shouting and shuffling behind me. Simu lifted Lebo to her chest. She attempted to drag me back with her, behind the safety of our fence. When I brushed her away, Simu tried to slap Abák's hindquarters to see if it would go, but Abák would not move. I could make out the sounds of men calling out to arm themselves with spears and to prepare. The elephant, ears flapping, trumpeting, charged down on us.

"'Run, Liloe!' Simu called to me, her voice cutting through the yells and cries.

"I stood by the young elephant's side and placed my hand on its head. The men all crouched, ready to fling their spears. Before they could, I opened my mouth and began to sing the song Lebo had sung earlier that day, the same blessing song Simu would sing to me that same night. I sang it the best way I knew and my voice never faltered. *May the children greet her knees. May she grow to be lucky. Be oretiti tree with the spread-out roots. May God bring you back.* I did not take my eyes off the mother elephant. Abák obeyed and ran to its mother. The calf was received with a sniff and a caress, before the mother scolded it with a lash of her trunk. The slap swept Abák underneath its mother's front legs, where it began to feed. That is when the mother elephant curled her trunk and bowed her head. Both elephants turned around and trod off up the hill to join their herd."

"I don't want to talk about the elephant," Serafim says. "I was wondering if we could go back to something you said earlier."

"What would you like to know?"

"I'm interested in the villagers' reaction when you returned with Lebo and the elephant. You stood your ground." He leans forward in his chair.

"Yes. They saw a power in me and called me a witch."

"You were always different by virtue of your skin colour, but the villagers attached some sort of magic to that difference. When were you first aware that your skin colour set you apart?"

"It has always been that way."

"I understand, but I was—"

"I have no power." I fumble with the ointment the doctors have left for me. The balm soothes the open sores that cover my neck, where the sun damages our skin most. I reach under my shawl to rub the cream behind my neck. I notice my hand shaking.

"You seem so certain of this, and yet I have spoken to many here who tell me you have saved them," Serafim says.

"People need to believe in something, someone. It is easier this way."

I turn for an instant to face him. His eyes do not move away from me when he offers a cigarette. I wave it off. He adjusts his recorder on the table before lighting a cigarette, squinting in a cloud of smoke.

"Do you have family in Brazil?"

Serafim shakes his head.

"Have you left someone behind?"

"No. I am alone," he says, and I know this is true.

"I know why you are here."

"I have made my intentions clear from the beginning," he says, and I hear the conviction in his voice. "I have never misled you."

"Yes, but what exactly do you need from me?"

"Your story," he says.

"I am telling you my story as stories should be told."

Serafim scratches the back of his head.

"I tell you I have no power, yet you are not convinced. Are you like the others? Are you searching for an angle? Because if you are, I am not here to be used in this way."

Serafim stands. "I need—"

I raise my hand to stop him. "I think I know what it is you need, what it is you search for. I know what power is, so let me make myself clear. I have been imprisoned in this hotel for years. Others have followed to lock themselves inside because it is safer here. If you want to tell the world why we are here, how it is we survive, then you must tell them in the words I use, not your own."

Serafim looks to the door and then reaches for his satchel.

"Stay. But speak slowly," I say. "Your accent is difficult for me."

"What should I call you? Your name . . . for the article."

"I have many names." I realize this is a riddle. "You can call me what they all call me here—a *branca*. Or you can use the last name given to me, P6."

I stop by the shutters that lead out to the balcony. I need air. I hear Serafim bending the notebook binding, ruffling some pages. I turn around just as Amalia appears at the entrance of my room. She is eight years old and dark. Her grin turns sour when she sees Serafim, smoking and sitting on the chair with his pencil in hand. She jumps into my bed and pulls the covers up to her chin.

Serafim knows Amalia's story. Like many before her, her mother found this place when she was a frightened young girl. She gave birth to Amalia here, in my room. The young mother died and her child became mine. Amalia is with me always. She tells me I am beautiful every day. Not with words, but in the way she looks at me and how she touches my face, her fingers crawling over my eyes, nose, cheeks, and throat. She hears me, but smiles to feel my voice through her fingertips. It is true that I have all my teeth, at least the ones that can be seen. I take a brush to them three times a day, sometimes four. A mix of seawater and sand is all I use. My hair remains golden, and curled tight to my head. It is difficult to catch my eyes or pin them down. I cannot control how they flick from side to side, and for this reason I cannot focus for too long. They are hard to read, and I like that.

"I was given the name Pó. It is the name I own now. Before that I was Liloe, a name my aunt Simu gave me. Amalia thinks Giz is a better name because my skin looks like chalk." I smile at her. She lifts the covers over her head.

"What were you named at birth?" he asks.

"I will not speak that name until it is time." Simu told me I must never call out the name I was given at birth or the spirits will think I am ready to be taken back to the place I came from, where I will be covered in darkness.

"I don't understand." He looks away, raking his fingers through his hair.

"When I am ready to leave this place."

"And you will know when that is?"

"No. I will only know when I am ready."

"I understand."

"I'm not sure you do. If you choose to sit and record my words, you must understand only one thing."

"What is that?"

I turn to look at the man before me, his skin warmed by the oil lamp next to his face, the other half of his face blacked out by shadow. Amalia holds her carved elephant in the air, pretending it is thundering through the brush.

"You say you come here to write of me, but all scribblers hope they will find the magic that everyone speaks of, that we albinos carry in us. You must listen to my words. You must promise to tell my story the way I have shared it with you."

"I am only interested in your story," he replies.

"You wrote an article over a year ago about an unknown tribe in Brazil."

"I did." I can hear the wooden chair creaking. The scribbler is leaning back.

"You became quite famous."

"That was not my intent," he says, stuffing his satchel with his notes and his recorder.

"Why do you run?" I ask.

Securing his bag over one shoulder, he places a cigarette in his mouth.

"When my questions become uncomfortable you pack your things to leave."

He flicks his lighter, takes a drag from his cigarette.

I hug myself tighter against the breeze. "All of us who live in the Grande Hotel are like everyone else. We carry the weight of what others fear or desire or do not understand. If you are like the other scribblers who have sat in that same chair, you'll believe my life is given value by the things I have done."

I pause a few seconds.

"You would be wrong."

Serafim

✴

As punishment for bringing the elephant to our village, Lebo and I did not eat that night. I can still see Koinet eating his bowl of ugali, the maize sticking to his fingers and sitting in the corners of his mouth, while my belly ached.

"You did not do as I asked today," Simu scolded us. "Instead of wood you brought an elephant, and with it, danger." Simu's worry forced me to turn away. I nudged closer to Lebo. Simu continued, "You must remember, it takes one day to destroy a house. To build a new house will take months, perhaps years."

"Did I break our house, Simu?"

"Quiet now," she said, gently laying leaves soaked in aloe and milk on my burning skin. She dragged a few leaves across my forehead. I rolled onto my back to let her continue. Everything outside was quiet, except for the insects singing and the katydids calling to one another.

"What will happen to the elephant?" I asked.

"It will grow to be big and strong."

I can picture us sleeping in the hut as if it was yesterday. Lebo faced the wall. I drew the cowhide over his shoulder and around my waist. Koinet lay close to us under another cowhide. Simu and Majuto lay at the opposite end of the hut. There was quiet for a while, but then I heard breathing sounds that came out of Majuto's nose. I felt Koinet creeping closer to me, trying to get warm. I wanted him to move away. My skin felt hot and sore. He pressed up against my back. I could not shake the heat of his breath warming my neck. His clenched fist hovered in front of my face. He opened his hand and I saw a ball of ugali, scraped from the sides of the pot. "You were brave, Cousin," he whispered. I took a bite and curled my tongue around the sweet taste. I reached over to place the rest between Lebo's lips.

❋

I press the recorder's Stop button.

NOTES: Friday, Oct. 14, 2016. Grande Hotel
— P6 - bold, strong, determined.

— Even as young girl, ~~possessed an early~~ understood
something of the way the world presented itself. "Did
I break our house?" Does not want to disappoint Simu.

— Simu = cared for Pó. Loved her. Protected her. Most
importantly, <u>guided</u> her as Liloe. How? By filling her head
with song and stories all meant to ~~calm her,~~ shield her,
make her feel safe/secure.

— Simu reassures her—your mother is always with you.
How does a child understand this?

— Still not certain why she chose story of elephant?

— Many questions raised regarding credibility of story.

— Pó almost playful with me. Perhaps her way of connecting?
Chose a mythical telling to draw me in? Her narrative is
working, but not able to believe her story, not fully. Often
difficult to separate what really happened from
embellishment.

— Dropped by big game outfitter near hotel. ~~Hunting on
upswing since animals returned after civil war.~~ Asked
about elephant behaviour. Highly unlikely for a wild calf
to behave in way Pó said—outfitter said "impossible."

— Pó insistent she doesn't have any special powers and yet
the details she seems most committed to suggest she
does. In her own words, she claims the power to tame
a mother elephant through her song? Highly unlikely. Why
so attached to telling this story in such a mythical way?
Maybe ~~wants~~ needs to believe in the perception of her

powers to understand why Simu would be so afraid for her, why Simu would send her away?

— Pó is eleven when supposed story occurred. Perhaps special power suggested in her story speaks to source of Simu's concern and reason for her exile—that she couldn't dissuade community from their beliefs about Pó. Or maybe it is Pó's insistence that villagers feared what they did not understand and this is what identified her as an outsider.

— Effect = draws me in and has a power over me—makes me want to believe.

— I am committed to reporting Pó's story as she tells it, while the journalist in me is challenged by story's credibility.

— Must not underestimate her. Off guard when she mentioned she had read my article on tribe in Brazil.

My damp shirt and underwear hang from a line I've stretched across my balcony. They do not move in the still night air. The moon hangs low. The patches of ocean I see peeking between apartment buildings are liquid mercury. Children at the corner erupt in laughter and howls as they smash beer bottles along the sidewalk. The same sounds as those I heard as a child on the streets of Florianópolis.

I top up my drink, reach for another cigarette, but the Marlboro pack is empty. I stand at the balcony, cup my hands around my mouth, and shout out to the kids. "Hey! Up here! I'm throwing down a hundred meticais rolled in an empty pack of cigarettes. First one to get me a pack and bring it up to my room will get paid." I throw the pack down. They elbow and claw at each other, the whites of their eyes the only thing I can barely make out. Before I can see who has been victorious, they scurry away together to the nearest store, the slap of their soles echoing through the empty street.

I was alone in the shack after my grandmother died. I would have been younger than Pó when she tamed her elephant. Only a few days after, I packed a few things in a plastic bag and made my way down the slope of the favela, a zigzag of lanes I knew well. I did so before someone claimed our shack and moved in.

At that age I did not ask questions. I didn't think it was possible to stand my ground and fight back. I don't think Pó ever felt that way. What made her feel bold enough to stand up to life? I can think back now as an adult and rationalize that life is random and uncertain, and there isn't always justice. All one is left with is the attempt to try and change the odds of any given circumstance. There is always uncertainty, but every so often there is a reward. But as a child, is one capable of such self-awareness, or have Pó's memories been gilded in a way, to protect her and the ones she loved?

"Senhor!" a boy yells up, his arm in the air holding what looks like a fresh pack of cigarettes.

"Well done! You're the winner!"

Ezequiel

A FLUORESCENT BULB FLICKERS. I lie in bed and turn to look out the window. The grape leaves are brown, curling and dropping off.

I want to escape the tangle of bedsheets. The weight of my body won't allow it and the strain is too much. *Breathe slow, deep.*

In 1973 I wanted to get as far away from Africa as possible, and Canada opened up to me then. Now all I do is flood my head with thoughts of that place long ago. The very process of thinking comes from a voice that has crept into my head, leaves a message, and then disappears.

"Ezequiel."

I hear the clicking of plates and cutlery against the stainless sink.

"Are you awake, Ezequiel?"

My hand trembles as I reach for the glass of water on my nightstand.

"I'll take care of that for you," the woman says, entering my room.

I clench the sheets at my side and try to tear them off.

The woman holds out her hands. And then I see the worry in her eyes and I know she is showing me she does not carry a weapon.

"What do you want with me?"

"I'm your home-care nurse. You said it was okay to let myself in."

Her face is beginning to come into focus.

"Magda," she says. She steps out of the room and returns with the Post-it note from the refrigerator's side. She holds up the yellow square. MAGDA.

I allow my head to sink back into the pillow. Magda holds the glass of water, opens her mouth and makes a sound to encourage me to do the same. She reminds me of a fish. She places the two small pills on my tongue, tips the glass so I can chase them down my throat with a gulp of water. The burning sensation will soon be replaced by a tingling in my arms. The heat will flush my insides—my chest, my neck, my head.

"I was just tidying up a bit. I'll put on a load of laundry, and then we can talk about how you're feeling."

Her Polish accent is strong for such a young woman. She keeps buzzing around the small room, leaving and coming back in, doing those small household chores that I don't care about. She talks to herself with everything she does.

"Would you like something to eat?" she asks, before sitting on my bed.

I inch away, faintly recalling doctors trying to explain memory distortions to me—the idea that a memory has already happened when it has not, thinking an old memory is a new one, combining two memories, or confusing the people in my memories.

"You won't be seeing me for three weeks," she says.

"You're not coming back?"

"Only for a few weeks. My father is not well in Poland. I need to fly home."

I cannot see Papa's face.

"I can still fly," I say.

"Where are you flying to?"

"Over the treetops, high above the jungle."

"And what do you see?" Magda says.

I shut my eyes, but she leans into me and I can feel her ear hovering over my lips.

"Mother Anke is at the bottom of the well."

It hurts to swallow my saliva.

"Papa Gilberto's boots are dirty," I mutter, the sobs choking my breath. "And the fire . . . my home is orange with fire."

✳

The smell of metal erupts from Macaco's breath when he sings, *God gave me the plan. I'm following through, going to build me a bridge.* The whir of helicopter rotors above—*chak chak chak chak.* Trees in the forest bend away from the spinning blades. My head is drowning in the faint cries of last breaths. Flies thick on the impaled head of a goat. The dead lie contorted, dredged in dust. A thud booms across my chest, the world turning on its end. I taste Armando's blood splatter. *Take me home,* he mumbles, legless, bleeding out. *Chak chak chak chak.* A ball of fire, its searing heat consumes Macaco and his men. I'm thrown into the sky, twisting against the blue. I will be in His beautiful hands. Armando has left this place, too. Quiet. An uncomfortable quiet. Facing blackened walls and scattered paper, I play the song that I have always known. A Portuguese soldier stands over me, the muzzle of his gun pressing against my temple . . .

I wake up. My body has cracked open and blood is running down my face and chest. I fumble in terror for some light, but I can't find a candle or a flashlight. I lie back down on my bed in the dark. Time has slipped by me. All that remain are fragments of memory.

It can't be blood. It's only a fever, the sweat squeezing out of my body, or perhaps what I feel crawling across my face and chest are insects, drawn to the beads of sweat like animals enticed by a watering hole. I try to get up. I fall to the ground and have to crawl in the dark. I don't want to stray too far from my bed. I feel a wave of fever coming on. I've had malaria before. I can hear my own breathing and I feel the fever rattling inside me.

I climb back onto the bed. My fingers clutch at the wet sheets and I strain my neck, pressing the back of my head down on the pillow. The attack is more violent than the ones before. I do not want to return to that place. I cry out in the darkness for Papa. I'm certain he is sitting outside, waiting for me.

"Papa!"

It's a new recording, he whispers, his voice tinkling like coins.

"Where are you, Papa?"

I make out the words *Rusalka, Dvořák.* I breathe in his day smell—tobacco and straw and horse.

The fever rolls in again like an ocean wave.

I can't swim. I'll drown. I grip the sheets to stay above the water.

I have to hold on, to keep thinking *it's only the fever, nothing more.*

It starts to rain in the room. The rain is pouring in and it is filling the room. I feel the bed floating before it begins to swirl in the water. I hold on tight, close my eyes and retch next to my pillow. I lift my head and a clarity emerges. There is no rain in the room. My bed is firmly set on the ground. The men have been lost.

It will only be a few minutes until the next wave finds me.

My bout of malaria lasted a good week or two. I'm not certain. I have been told that six weeks ago I entered the camp as a prisoner. None of Macaco's men had made it. The last one had been dragged into the jungle and shot. I think of Armando looking to heaven.

Here, I fought back. When they woke me every morning in the dark to get the kitchen ready for breakfast, I would punch something, whatever was close by. I refused to do anything at first. I wouldn't let them have power over me.

The surge of my rebellion has lessened. Still, I do their bidding reluctantly. At noon, they give me bread and soup of cassava leaves and okra. I eat my first bowl of hot soup in the open, away from the other men. I sit there wiping the rain off my face and listening to it crashing through the branches, hitting the canvas tents till they are soaked and the ground turns black. I focus my attention on the gushing torrent that breaks down the ground to form small rivers across the clearing. I eat my soup and my insides grow warm.

I ignore the movement in the camp, of soldiers and militia. They are mostly commissioned soldiers and assimilados. Most are white, but there are also black soldiers, who carry out orders against cousins and brothers. They seem uncertain of me, keep their distance, but a few of the men in our tent have shown some kindness: bringing me food, urging me to eat something or drink, or offering a kind word.

August 1966. On the calendar pinned to the tent wall, the twenty-eighth is circled in pen, and I think how odd it is for there to be so much rainfall in August. The heavy rains only begin in October, if we are lucky.

At night I pile dishes outside the mess tent. I know from the scraps what I will eat later, after all the soldiers have eaten their meals and after I have washed all the dishes. Today it is green bananas and beans, cabbage and onions, goat, I think, swimming in a thick broth. In the mornings, far earlier than anyone else gets up, I flush out the latrines, which are nothing more than holes at the edge of the camp. I pour buckets of water in the ditches to dilute the stench before lining them with moss, ready for another day.

I'm not certain of our exact location, except I know we are near marshland and the Zambezi River, not far from a place where engineers are looking to build a dam. Government officials often take Portuguese soldiers from the camp to escort them to the site. The camp is erected close to a makeshift airstrip. The Portuguese run the camp. No prisoners remain. I have heard they have been transported elsewhere, to prisons in bigger cities. I'm not allowed to go near the airstrip, but I can hear the hum of aircraft landing or taking off. On the other side is a swamp bordered by mangroves, their roots anchored on nothing. I'm told if I'm not careful I will slip inside and be trapped in the mangroves' underwater cages. There are breezy days when I must cover my mouth and nose from the rot that sweeps across the camp.

Sheets and a pillow are the one luxury I am happy to have. I share a tent with six men who are relegated to a separate tent. I am the youngest at sixteen and forced to do the most menial tasks. I'm not quite like them and they are unsure of me. I am not afraid.

"You are to be repatriated—reinstated into normal society," the lieutenant told me shortly after my malaria broke.

"I'm going home?" Confused by my own question.

"You have no home, Ezequiel. When this war is over you'll adjust to your new life. It is clear you are educated. Your Portuguese is too precise. You were raised by whites on a mission, I believe."

"How do you know?" I held my breath, pressed down any recollection of the place.

"Malaria is like liquor. It reveals things."

"I don't know what you're talking about."

"You called out to Papa Gilberto—your father at the mission. You are one of us," he said.

I don't trust the lieutenant's protection. It sounds like he knew Papa Gilberto, but it could be a trap. I certainly don't feel I belong to anyone or anything. He thinks that a change of place, removing me from Macaco's group, will make me "normal." I walk into the barracks and feel as if nails are being hammered into my head. The tent's ceiling is dark. I bind a tea towel around my head and lie down awhile. My eyes struggle to become familiar with my surroundings. I splash some cold water on my face and look at the small mirror that hangs on the tent wall. I notice facial hair for the first time, and I feel distant from the face I see.

A fresh uniform, a bar of glycerin soap, and a towel are at the foot of my bed. Next to them is the beret and a pair of new boots. It is the uniform of the Caçadores, the elite light infantry soldiers of the Portuguese army. I'm not certain what to do with it all.

Tucked in the towel is a toothbrush, some toothpaste, a straight razor and shaving soap, hair grease, and a tortoise-shell comb. These gifts mean something. I'm not sure what I have done.

That evening, a nick under my chin and one below my ear, my beret slightly askew, the way the other soldiers wear it. Augusto, the cook, enters the tent and whistles. A tall man with a slightly hunched back, he tames his silver hair with what the other men in our tent joke is pork grease. The smell of him keeps everyone constantly hungry.

"Didn't need any spit with that polish," he grins.

Those are his first words to me and I'm caught off guard. His smile brings me back to happier times at the mission, where so many of the workers drew me in with their warm gestures that made me feel like I belonged with them. Shame overwhelms me. I turn away and am confronted by the lieutenant standing by the barracks entrance. He allows Augusto to slip away.

"I see you've found the new uniform. I have your orders," he says, taking my beret off my head. "You have no need for this tonight," he says.

The lieutenant is well-dressed this evening. His skin looks pasty, no matter how pressed his uniform or how perfectly parted his hair. He knows my secrets.

"We are expecting a very important man tonight—a very powerful man. I have recommended you to be his personal assistant. Do you understand me, Ezequiel?" A dribble of spit runs down from the corner of his lip. "Understand?" he says, pressing a cloth to his swollen cheek.

"Yes," I say, and I feel relief that this man has delivered me once again.

"Good. You are in his complete command. You are to do everything this man tells you. If he asks you to wipe his ass, you do so. You smile while you do it. The last thing you want is to make him angry."

"Why?"

"You don't want to find out," he says, straightening his shirt cuffs. They are not rolled up above his elbows the way he normally wears them. "If anything goes wrong, if you hear

any complaints or if he appears dissatisfied, I need you to—"
He places a hand on my shoulder. His nose almost touches
mine. "Take these," he says, and places some official-looking
identity documents in my hands. "I will come for you when
he arrives."

"His name?" I ask.

The lieutenant hears me but only walks away. He stops at
the tent's opening, his back to me.

All I do is hold my breath.

At night, the heat makes life difficult. You wake up drenched and
begin the day that way. The tsetse flies gorge on blood and mosquitoes make sleeping impossible. I remain dressed and wait
alone in my tent to be called. Some of the soldiers are discussing
what went wrong in combat, how they lost three men, boys
really. They were Azorean. By their tone, it sounds things could
have been worse.

Papa Gilberto taught me about Portugal and all its colonies
spread across the world. I knew about the Azores Islands, Goa,
Macau, and other Portuguese colonies in Africa. There were
colourful maps. He used a book he had in his office to explain
the history of Mozambique, and he read from the book like a
teacher giving a lesson. There was no pride in his voice. I once
asked him if he was Portuguese. Without taking a breath he
replied, *No, I'm Mozambican.* His family could be traced back
three hundred years, but why they came was something he

didn't like to talk about. Slavery. Only once did he speak of how his relatives, people he no longer knew or had much in common with, now lived off the land they had stolen.

I hear a convoy of trucks drive into the clearing. I'm sitting on my lower bunk, facing the wall, but there is still no relief of my migraine.

I'm not certain how long I have been lying on my cot when the lieutenant nudges me. In a daze, I wipe the sweat from my forehead, careful not to mess my hair. He says nothing. I simply follow him outside. I take a quick look in the mirror. My hair is parted. The grease has darkened my sandy hair to a brown.

"*Pronto*. Remember one thing, only speak when asked to. Keep it brief. Do as you are told."

The lieutenant leaves me at the entrance to a newly erected tent, a little way from the cluster of tents in the camp. I step inside and the largest man I have ever seen blocks me. He is bald. The light in the tent reflects off his smooth head. His arms are crossed in front of his chest and he does not move.

"Abel, leave us alone," a voice says.

Abel moves aside and bends to exit.

Without Abel blocking my view, I'm struck by the tent's luxurious interior: a mahogany desk and chair, travel trunks, a full bed with linens suspended off the floor and completely draped with mosquito netting. The floor is covered with Persian rugs, layered over each other. A small table is set next to the bed. On it are a candle and some books. Near it, on a longer table, I see a plate made of china and decanters of wine and liquor and an assortment of goblets made of cut crystal. My head is pounding.

"Don't mind Abel." The deep voice emerges from behind a screen that has been set up in the corner of the tent. A military uniform is draped over the screen and in front of it is a porcelain washbasin and jug.

"He's harmless. Except to those I tell him to hurt." He gives a half-hearted chuckle. "I cut off his tongue," he says, and I'm not sure if I'm expected to react. "He's very good at keeping secrets," the man says, emerging from behind the screen cinching his robe across his waist. "What's your name?" A small breeze could shift the mosquito netting and catch fire.

"Zeca," I say.

He walks up to me, and I notice his limp. One leg is shorter than the other and the heel never touches the ground. I try to avert my eyes, but he is upon me before I can look up.

"The lieutenant said your name was Ezequiel. I don't like names that are shortened. It cuts a man in half. But you are still a boy, I see." His eyes shine the colour of an escudo, coppery and unreal. His sideburns almost meet with the ends of his full moustache, the tops of which are waxed and twisted to a point.

He is a tall man, six foot two or so. So pale, and his teeth are white and straight. The sweltering heat of the tent only makes the smell of him that much stronger, a mix of freshly sawn wood and musk.

"Your lieutenant's breath reeks, but I can see he chose wisely." He measures me with a smile. I want to defend the lieutenant, but I hold my tongue.

He pinches my chin and turns my face away. "Mulatto," he says, and I hear the displeasure in the word. His hand drops. His power frightens me. The men I had spent time with in the bush knew I could read and write. The workers I was raised with in the mission, all black, also recognized my social status—son of white missionaries.

"A mulatto may serve my purpose. I need a shadow." He steps to the table, where his meal has been finished. "Someone to do my bidding before I even know what I want." He looks down at his plate. "It's so hard to find that kind of *understanding* in this place. But can you be trusted?"

I move to the table and pick up the plate and cutlery, clear the table for him before he sits down. I am too afraid to do anything wrong. I walk carefully, terrified of tripping. The weight of his plate steadies my hand. I am terrified to look at him. I have seen how brutal a man can be, and this man holds such power.

"They need us. They turn us into beasts, but they need us. The problem is there are too many of them. A burden. They fuck like rabbits and we're the ones who need to look after them. Without us they're useless. They just don't know it."

His words ring in my ears and make me feel dirty. I leave the tent and drop the plates outside the opening. A slight breeze whispers through the jungle. I return to the warmth inside the tent. The man sits in his chair at the table. He holds a glass of green liquid over a candle. He swirls it slowly over the flame, his eyes focused on the task.

"I'm told you like music," he says.

It is not a question, and I do not respond. I do not know who told him this or how it is anyone knows. I play my harmonica only when alone and under my covers, and even then I do so quietly. I can't chance them taking it away from me.

"The leather box on top of the trunk," he says.

I make my way over to it and open a portable record player. All the metal parts are gold-plated and the motor board a dark polished wood. The winding handle is attached to the outside, and inside the lid is a collection of five albums. I slip one out of its jacket, *Kind of Blue* by Miles Davis, and place it on the turntable. I crank the arm. The sound emerges into the suffocating heat trapped in the tent.

I have never heard such discordant sounds fitting so perfectly together.

"Come here," he says, his eyes slightly closed as he swirls his drink over the flame. "You are to call me Commander. Do you understand?"

He offers me his drink. "Absinthe," he says. I take the warm glass from his hand, my fingers brushing across his hairy knuckles. His nails are buffed and appear wet.

The liquid is slightly bitter, but the taste of anise comes through.

"You like the green fairy, do you?"

I nod and give him back the glass. Reaching up, before I can take a step back, the Commander's thumb is smudging a dribble from the corner of my mouth. My lips do not tremble; they are numb.

"Not easy to come by, but anything can be bought, even in this hell." He again hovers the glass over the flame.

The hot liquid is burning its way down my throat. I feel the flames licking the insides of my stomach. I close my eyes for a second, but the sound of shattering glass forces them open. The Commander holds the broken glass in his hand. The absinthe has spilled over the candle and doused the flame. I grab the towel from the wash basin and press it to his hand. With my other hand I remove the shard embedded in his palm. He does not appear to feel a thing, simply tilts his head back and closes his eyes. I curl his fingers over the towel, urge him to hold on to stop the flow. I dampen a cloth in his basin and begin to wipe his hand. He has the five-dots tattoo that many of the soldiers do. The five dots are arranged like the dots on a dice, spaced between his thumb and forefinger.

"I think you'll work out fine," he says. His eyes, although half-closed, are on me. I cannot help but think he is testing me and I dare not look away.

"Bring me my razor," he says. I return to him with a dry towel and the razor he requested. "And another candle and that bottle of ink on my desk." I do as I'm told. I place these on the table. He burnishes the tip of the razor over the flame.

"Give me your hand," he says.

Inside the warm glow of the tent I give in to his power over me.

The Commander dips the right angle of the straight razor into the ink. He presses the point to the top of my hand, near the base of my thumb. I feel the pinprick of heat, the moment the drop of my blood mixes with the ink, and I hear him say, "Half-blood."

"These dots represent the five shields of Portugal. It will protect you. You can trust President Salazar," he whispers. "Only he can free us." He whispers "Salazar" as he pricks my skin for the second time with the corner of the blade.

I close my eyes and let him press the tip of the blade three more times. Each time he presses the point of the blade down, there is an urge to take a step back. He whispers a word with each prick he makes: "power," "wisdom," and "loyalty." The heat radiates on my skin as the ink mixes with my blood.

He takes the same cloth I had used to clean his wound and finds a clean corner. He lays it over my fresh tattoo and presses down, as if sealing our pact.

"Loyalty is the most important," he says, almost dreamlike. He draws in his breath, hesitates. His yellow eyes hold me in a trance. "In Africa death is always close by. The heat. The rot."

The Commander grabs my arm and tugs me closer. I look away but his hot breath fills my ear.

"The blacks are coming. And when they do, I'll be ready for them."

The months pass and I am content to move from camp to camp with the Commander and Abel. I have picked up details of the Commander along the way; have overheard some of the men of high rank call him Commander Anselmo Fonseca. I've been able to piece together that he is a commander of the Polícia Internacional e de Defesa do Estado, what they called PIDE. The group rounds up snitches, sometimes women, who are offered money or certain positions of power in exchange for secrets. If these incentives don't work, PIDE resorts to torture.

The Commander is a powerful man in the colonial police and he oversees Portugal's counter-insurgency operation. As a young man he was hand-picked by the head of PIDE. The Commander spoke highly of this man, saw him as a mentor, a father figure, who recognized a quality of character in him that his own father had not. I know this because the Commander goes into long tirades. Anger spewing from him, he transforms into his father. *You'll never amount to much, not with your deformity. You need to build character.* This mentor recognized how the Commander had turned his deformity into a strength, harnessing his resentment into a cold ruthlessness. In 1956, this man dispatched the Commander to Mozambique to head the secret police here. "*Gave me this shithole*" is how the Commander describes it. "Saw something in me and rewarded me with this misery."

The Commander turned forty-eight a month ago. There was a small celebration in his tent. He is not married and has no children. I saw a couple of drunk soldiers making sexual gestures that had them bent over with laughter. There are days when I still feel I am walking in circles in the forest with Macaco and his men. I attach myself to the Commander, even though his violent racism leaves me shaky, often feeling empty. There is the half of me that he resents, but I need to believe that I'm growing stronger under his protection. The other men do not toy with me now. Those I share a tent with look to the cook for cues. Augusto smiles and nods when I enter our sleeping quarters. There is concern in his voice when he speaks to me in front of the other men. There is no judgment in his words. He understands. They all do. Perhaps this is why I leave our tent ashamed, discomfited, all of us players in a degrading sport.

Many soldiers are out every day planting land mines, hundreds of them, added to the million or more that are already out there or will come eventually. I don't understand the verb "plant" because I think of flowers and vegetables, things that bring beauty to the world. I think of all the civilians who will lose their limbs or lives—farmers, women, and children who are tending gardens, planting food, harvesting crops, or simply strolling to the river to fetch water. In shallow holes, soldiers plant land mines, and the same holes become graves for those who step on them.

I have seen them training near camp, on their knees digging. Carefully, they handle the metal casings, activate them before lowering the discs in the bed of dirt and covering them over. Filled with tiny metal darts called flechettes, they are lethal. I have seen a soldier who did it wrong—his body shredded to a pulp.

I am allowed to shower and change before going to the Commander's tent to prepare his room and serve him dinner. I look forward to this time. I try to get there early so I can drown myself in the music called jazz that he likes to listen to as he eats.

The Commander comes in late. His food has gone cold and I move to clear the table. I will quickly get them to heat up some dinner for him.

"We leave tomorrow night," he says, before he notices me balancing the plate with its metal dome, wine glass in hand. "I have no appetite," he says, and sits down heavily in his chair. I lower the plate onto the table. "My feet are sore," he says, yawning.

I pour water into the wash basin from the matching jug. I place the basin by his feet. Sitting cross-legged, I look up at the Commander as I unlace his boots. I lift his bare foot and place it over the basin. I wash his foot, gently at first, with soap and water. I begin to rub the arch, then work my way around his toes, his heel, before my fingers reach his ankle. I keep my eyes closed. It allows me to separate what my hands are doing from the pleasure of the jazz filling the tent. The heat is dizzying.

The Commander flinches, ever so slightly. I open my eyes as he leans forward. He brushes the outside of his thumb against my cheek. I want to shake his hand from my face. I pat dry his foot, wipe each toe, one by one. I grab the ankle of his other foot, the deformed one, and lift it over the washbasin. He slips down lower until the crook of his neck rests on the back of the chair. His mouth opens slightly, and I catch the silver flash of his metal fillings. He lets out a low groan. I keep rubbing his twisted foot, but there is a sudden splash of water as his foot drops in the basin.

"You can leave now," he says.

He stares at the entrance of his tent where a girl, a teenager, stands shivering. Set against her dark skin, a white orchid is tucked behind her ear. I stand and she does not raise her eyes to meet mine. I walk past her and catch her scent—sweet, like the smell of freshly cured tobacco leaves. She is one of the girls from the nearby fields.

I went to bed imagining the young tobacco picker, naked except for the flower in her hair. In my dream she swayed to the jazz music and I blushed with excitement. I am woken in the still, dark morning by the faint trace of her smell. I am soaked. The night birds singing are soon drowned out by the sounds of helicopter rotors.

There is no light, only a sliver of moon. I dress and make my way over to the Commander's tent. It is my duty to prepare him for the morning: dump his chamber pot, help him shave and dress, serve him breakfast. I know from the sound of helicopters and the convoy coming into the camp that my day will be spent carefully packing everything in Commander Fonseca's tent before Abel loads it all into a truck. It will be sent to the new location and unloaded to the Commander's specifications. It will all be waiting for him before we arrive.

"Are you all right, Commander?" I am aware that I never speak to him or greet him in this way, but this morning, he is sitting at his table and he strains his eyes. It's as if he is in a faraway place. "Do you need help, sir?"

The Commander rubs his eyes. I see blood on his hands. I move closer and see that he is naked. His body is covered in blood.

"Are you hurt, sir?" I ask, but the Commander twists the ends of his moustache as if performing a calculation in his head. "Let me help you, Commander."

The Commander looks down and sees all the blood. He turns to me with a look begging me to explain. I don't move. The Commander gets up and staggers to the basin. He washes his hands, slowly at first, but then he becomes more brutal in his scrubbing, almost frantic.

A papaya is in the middle of the table that is covered in maps. Some cashews are strewn around the fruit. Flies jump off and on. They land on the two empty glasses on the table, one of which is toppled. Its spilled contents blot the maps, the green fairy. I glance at the stained sheets again, at a dark, deep red, almost black spot, and I see the knife.

I scan the room and now I catch the pale underside of a girl's foot at the edge of the Commander's dressing screen. The buzzing of flies grows louder as I get close.

"The love of war is a passion like any other. You love soldiers as you love women—to madness."

Her body is curled up. Her hands clutch at her stomach, but her eyes are wide open and her head is turned up with parted lips.

"They must be kept in line." The Commander's mouth twitches.

"Sir?"

"They can't hide."

I place a fresh towel near the basin. Then I begin to strip the bed of its stiffened sheets. I yank at the mosquito netting till it falls down into a pile. I bundle it all in my arms and then drape it over the girl.

The Commander mutters to himself. "These tribes are always fighting. The Senas go at the Changanes, who go after the Makonde. Let them. The fewer there are of them, the quicker this war will be over."

He catches me looking at him and seems dazzled, his eyes riveted on me. I am his shadow and an accomplice to something vile. Again.

Pó

THE CHILDREN'S PLAYROOM was chosen because the door has a lock, and it is not as damaged as the other rooms. The plaster on most walls has been torn down to get at copper pipes. Much of the hotel was stripped of wires, and wooden floors have been ripped up for firewood. All that remains is a shell.

Ophelia watches over the children. She is patient with them, gentle with their needs. She understands what it is to grow up an albino at the Grande Hotel. It is her home now. Lately, she has been bold enough to slip away from the hotel at night. It worries me. She is sixteen, and I know that she sneaks out to visit with men at the bars and the billiards in Beira. She pencils in her eyebrows and dyes her hair black. I understand her reasons; all a girl wants at her age is to fit in, the freedom to feel there is only one way things can go. She takes risks, lost in the idea that there is nothing beyond her own experience. The men give her money. I do not judge her, I simply worry.

There are seven albino children in the playroom. The youngest is five, the oldest, twelve. A few of them sit colouring or practising their letters. An NGO from the capital visits twice a year to supply them with eyeglasses, but still their faces press up close to their books. The NGO uses the term persons with albinism or PWAs when referring to people like me. I appreciate the growing resistance to the word *albino*, and part of me is sensitive to the change, but I tell them I am of a different generation and am not wounded by it.

Ophelia stands at attention by the beds as four other children hop from one mattress to the next. They wrap themselves in the mosquito netting and swing from cot to cot. They land and a small cloud of dust lifts and sparkles in the shafts of sunlight that stream through the shutters. Amalia plays with the children. She is the only dark-skinned child her age here in Block B. She reaches into her pocket and draws out an elephant carving. It is one of the gifts Ezequiel gave me. I have given it to Amalia. The story that inspired it is her favourite. She holds the carving in her hand, her arm straight and raised. One of the boys grabs for it. Two other children reach up and clamour to hold it. The boy elbows the other children away, toppling them off the cot onto the floor. He is left standing alone with Amalia, his fingers crawling up her wrist. She stretches, holds her treasure high in the air.

I am tired. As I climb the curved staircase on the way back to my room, my hand is guided by the iron railing that was once there. It was torn out long ago and sold, like everything else in this once grand hotel. My mind still sees it there, at the top of the stairs. I remove my eyeglasses and the staircase is unclear. My mind fills in the blanks.

Using the walls for support, I walk down the dark hall to my room. I ignore the squatters cooking their food and smoking in the hallway. They reach out to me, try to grab the hem of my shuka or dare to touch my feet. I have learned to keep walking. My room will be cool and my bed soft. I will be alone. Down the dark hall I make out the shape of a figure smoking. The man sees me approaching and his posture stiffens. The man bows slightly as I near and I know it is Serafim.

"*Bom dia*," he says.

"You are early," I say, putting on my eyeglasses. I walk into my room feeling good about the pink sari draping around my neck that once belonged to Fatima. Serafim knocks on the inside wall before he enters. I do not turn to greet him right away.

I catch him placing a jar on the table next to the chair.

"I hope you don't mind. I brought some cream for you." He raises his hand to his neck. He digs into his bag and pulls out a chocolate wrapped in colourful foil. "And a chocolate for Amalia."

I give Serafim a sly smile. "That child's affections cannot be bought. Sit, please," I say, gesturing to the chair.

I lean my shoulder against the window frame, looking out. By the sound of it he has dragged the chair closer to the table before sitting. There is the snap of an elastic band, which most likely holds his notebook closed. He leafs through some sheets and I hear the scratch of pencil on paper—he is writing the date next to the word *NOTES*. I have seen it before. I inhale and close my eyes, the familiar sounds taking me back to before he'd lie down to sleep—my soldier writing on his own scraps of paper.

"When did you first know you were good with words?"

"It's the one thing I've always done well." Serafim nibbles at the arm of his eyeglasses. He waits a few seconds. "After my grandmother died, I did not speak. For months I tried, but the sounds never took shape. It was my teacher who encouraged me to write things down instead." He chuckles to himself. "That's how those words and first phrases presented themselves, on paper. And I felt free."

"Have you ever tried to write your story down?"

Serafim wets his lips and I think he looks like a hungry man.

I tap my head to make it clear I hold everything inside of me. "When words are written," I say, "they can't be changed. If those same words swim in my head, I can always make them do what I ask."

I take in the shape of him, sitting comfortably in the chair. He wears a linen shirt that remains dry. He is not shaven, but his hair is greased and parted on the side. As he readies himself, his expression is soft, an invitation that draws me in. I want to tell him everything, but I am not a young girl, and I know what it is to hold back.

✳

One night, when I was thirteen, Simu nudged me awake. Koinet and Lebo were sleeping on the raised platform, under their skins, while Majuto slept on his back, his head on his wooden pillow.

"Get up, Liloe," Simu said, rolling me over onto my back.

Outside, the warmth of the rain struck me. The moon was out, and strange shadows were cast across the ground. Simu's ankles were covered in mud. Her shuka clung to her body. She held out a sack.

"Simu?"

"You must leave tonight, Liloe," she said, grabbing me and holding me tight. "I have watched over you with love and care. But the others will harm you and I cannot protect you from them. You are no longer safe here. I will not let you stay." She cupped my face in her hands. "You will go to the place your mother knew well. I am sending you to the city, to a great friend of your mother's. Your mother followed the river to the city a few times to sell jewellery to this woman. She trusted her. You will be safe there. There is a letter in this bag. I do not understand the words, but once you arrive, you must show the paper to someone there. There are coins and food in the bag as well." Simu turned over a large gourd covered by hide. Underneath were my mother's beaded collars and earrings.

"You must go, but wear your mother's things proudly. Use them wisely."

I preferred to travel in the dark. The moonlight guided me and comforted me. It was also safer to do so. The animals were not hungry, people were more easily avoided, and the sun did not beat down on my skin. I was heading to the large city near the sea.

When I grew hungry, I trapped a few small fish in my shuka and swallowed them whole. They swam down my throat. The worms I dug up from the riverbed tasted of mud. They too were slippery when I swallowed. I held my stomach and sang the song to the fishes swimming and the worms wriggling in my belly. When I noticed the signs that a village was close, I moved away. I listened for predators and kept my distance from lions—remained calm, never turned my back, and never ran. With other animals, like baboons, I made myself appear bigger by raising my arms over my head and making noise. The thoughts of food and water and animals and shelter crowded out thoughts of Simu and my home.

From a distance I saw a large stone where I knew I could

find shade. As I drew nearer, I could see it was not a rock but a truck. It must have swerved into a huge baobab. A shrub had grown through the floor into the front seats. I scanned the plain. It was rough and dusty—a dull brown landscape—and everything seemed to have faded away. The people in this truck had been lost, stuck in the middle of nowhere under a burning sun. From the condition of the truck's metal, it may have been there for years. As a child, I had seen a few of these machines from a distance, kicking up a long trail of dust. They never came close.

I needed rest. I crawled into the back seat. The shade from the roof felt good. I closed my eyes and slept.

I found a bag tucked under the seat. Inside were some men's clothes—long-sleeved shirts and trousers. I could use these to cover my head and neck. Underneath the clothes were some papers, held together in packets with wire. I couldn't read the scribbles written in these books and pages, but I thought the paper would start a strong fire. My fingers touched something smooth and cool in the bag—a pair of men's boots. I did not hesitate—the soles of my feet were cracking. I slipped on the boots. They were big, but my toes felt like they were dipping into a cold stream. I held back my tears. *Do not be afraid,* I heard in my head, and I knew that Simu and my mother were with me.

I had counted over thirty moons since I had left my village, and I feared there would be more moons than I could count before I reached the city. There were days when I felt I was no closer, as if I was walking in circles, but I pushed ahead. I ate berries. I no longer had the strength to dig for roots.

My feet began to vibrate with the ground. I climbed up to the first branch of the nearest tree. It was high enough to see the train coming. Steam and black smoke breathed from its head. I slipped down and ran through the trees and shrubs, I ran to the edge of the bush. Peeking through the shadows, I could see the train speeding along the plain. I could see people riding its roof or sitting in open parts of its cars, their legs dangling out over the edge. I was too hungry to be fearful. I ran towards the serpent that would take me to the great city by the sea.

In the distance, the train slowed down. A small herd of elephants crossed the tracks. I was thankful that I did not have time to think. I ran fast, my boots kicking the back of my heels. I threw my bag into one of the cars just as it jolted forward. I grabbed hold of a metal bar and swung my wobbly legs and body up onto the wooden floor. I dragged myself to crouch between large, ropy squares. The train's movement travelled up my back to my neck and head. With every gentle turn I tilted onto my side. It was dark inside the car, except for the lines of light that squeezed between the wooden walls. I sank back and pressed my hands against the bales of sisal to steady myself. The train gained speed. After a while, my heart did not beat so fast and my breathing steadied.

It took me quite a while to grow accustomed to the sounds

and the movement. I could not look down because the grasses blurred, but if I looked across, out into the plain, it was as if all trees and mountains were standing still. Everything had a shape to it, even when sand grains rose in the wind, dulling the sun. I crossed through low scrub that stretched far away into the distance where the purple thumbprints of mountains smudged the edge of the sky.

With my eyes half-closed, I passed patches of green where wild dogs chased the train. It was only when I neared the coast, and my trance began to obscure the shoreline, that I had no energy left for excitement. I let sleep take hold of me.

The train pulled up by a long house. A pair of man's legs dangled from the roof of the train. The man threw his bag to the ground, then jumped down and ran off. I stepped out onto the slanted concrete platform. A woman balancing a shapeless bundle on her head stacked a basket of chickens on top of a sack of dried fish. A man in uniform began to shake his arms and raise his voice at her. I looked away. I had seen hunters but never men dressed in uniforms with guns across their backs. All the jittering and knocking during my travels had made my stomach weak, but all was forgotten when I saw the city houses, square and tall, with windows going up three high. Their fronts were painted a brilliant white, and I thought if I pressed up against their walls I would disappear like a chameleon.

✽

"But you were only thirteen," Serafim says. "You must have felt so alone in the big city. Were you scared?"

"I'm not sure."

"What went through your mind when you arrived?"

"I didn't know what to expect and it was all new to me. I was tired, but I do remember feeling there was a place for me in that city."

"What made you feel that way?"

"Simu's words. She knew I could find peace in that place, the way my mother had."

"Did you?"

I take a deep breath, fill up my lungs until they ache. I exhale, slowly.

✳

I allowed all the people to stream around me. Through the high fence I saw two-wheeled vehicles everywhere, trundling slowly past. Women's dresses and headscarves fluttered, orange and violet and blue. Other people had stepped off the train and pushed me further into the city in a swell. They carried with them parcels and baskets on their heads. Words were spoken, some shouted and yelled. Not in Maa, my language, but in Swahili, a language I had heard when travelling hunters or neighbouring tribes passed through our village. I also heard people speaking in English, or what I thought was English, words Simu had used, words my mother had taught her after travelling to the city. Night was dropping and I saw the faint moon full. My shuka was stiff with sweat and dust. It cracked when I moved.

I reached for the small slip of paper Simu had given me. I unfolded it. I could not read it and needed help. But who could I trust? I walked along one of the streets, keeping close to the walls of the large homes. I did not notice if they saw me differently. They did not point or stare at my difference. They did not cross the road to avoid brushing against me. The people seemed so busy moving from one place to the next. I wanted to find a tree to sleep under, but short walls of concrete surrounded the trees. I would not feel safe sleeping out in the open in the middle of this city I did not know. Perhaps if I breathed softly, and just picked a direction, I would find my way.

"You are lost," a deep voice said, in Maa.

He stepped out from the shadow of an entranceway. Oh, he was tall and elegant, dressed as a lion warrior, his red-checked shuka draped across his ebony shoulders. His hair was the same red as his shuka.

"Do not be afraid," he said, leaning against his staff. I could see his white teeth as he spoke. He was not much older than me.

I offered the note with Simu's scribbles to him. "Can you help me?"

"Oh, the crazy Goan?" he said, and urged me to follow him.

"You know this woman?"

"Everyone knows Fatima."

I could not tear my eyes away from the way he walked, balancing his stride with his hunting staff. Even in the false light that glowed from the houses, there was something gracious in the way his body moved.

"We are here," he said, handing back the slip of paper. He smiled. "Would you like me to stay near?"

I wanted him to stay, but I shook my head, releasing him. He disappeared around one of the jagged corners.

The house had grilled windows, balconies, and an Arab door painted the colour of sorghum berries. I slapped at it. I did it again, and then slipped down to the ground, exhausted.

I heard a click. A woman said something I did not understand. Her straight black hair fell over her shoulders. Streaks of silver framed her face. She was trying to hit me with a broom handle, shouting words I could not understand.

I was untethered and there was no way of attaching myself to anything. I was ready to give up, leave, when I remembered what Simu had said. I opened my bag and pulled out my mother's necklace. I flattened the beaded necklace against my neck and chest.

The woman pointed her red fingernail at my necklace. "Namunyak," she whispered, before covering her mouth with her trembling fist.

"My mother," I said.

The woman caressed the intricate beadwork, traced her

fingers along it. "E-silá?" she said, the Maa word for daughter. She opened her door wide.

❊

As Serafim records my words and scribbles his notes, he is quiet. I look down at my bare feet. They are whiter than the rest of me—my soles smooth as beach stones. For most of my life I have protected them with boots; always men's boots because they are made better. I no longer run, or even walk long distances. My hands do all the work. Amalia often says, "Your hands are not as pretty as your feet, Alma." She calls me the Portuguese word for soul, and it pleases me. But a poor soul I am—two of my fingernails were crushed pounding corn for ugali, and they never grew back. The skin around my fingers is hard and yellow. Bleach no longer reddens my hands or makes them itch. I am immune to its bite. This is not true for other parts of my skin, which are covered in lesions from the sun. This condition is shared by many of us who live in this hotel. Often these marks do not go away but change, becoming darker and more sinister. I cover these markings so that others like me are not alarmed. Amalia is the only one who sees my open sores, and she ministers to them as if playing a game. I love her for it. And after I tell Amalia the stories of my life, I remind her that I am also grateful that I can still lay my hands on children's heads and feel their hair. I spend my days soothing their blistered skin.

Serafim slips his pencil behind his ear, buries it in his hair. He sets the recorder atop the small table, next to his ashtray, trapping my words inside the metal box.

"I followed the river," I whisper to myself, turning my back to the grounds and the whale breaching beyond the muddy waters of the Buzi River.

"And *was* she crazy?"

I am annoyed by the question. "The city could have swallowed me up, but Fatima gave me a home."

"How long did you stay with her?" Serafim sits on the edge of his seat, his elbows resting on his knees. His hands are held together as if in prayer. I have given him only bare facts. I want to say, *I held her for her last breath.*

"Almost two years in Dar es Salaam. At first it was difficult to speak to her. I only spoke Maa, but she had come from Goa and spoke Portuguese and Konkani. She came to Dar es Salaam to marry a merchant, who himself was Goan and Catholic. But he drank and put her to work like a servant in his shop. She learned Swahili. The few words she knew in Maa she had learned from my mother. Fatima said it was best to teach me one language— Portuguese. She said it was the only language God understood and it would serve me well *no Jardim do Éden*, she used to say. No one would bother us there. 'It is high on a mountain, a place where the four rivers meet.'"

"Was that Mount Gorongosa?" Serafim asks.

I close my eyes and nod. "The city turned ugly. Soldiers in

Dar were getting ready for their turn to cross the border and liberate themselves from colonial power. Fatima said to keep my distance. Their war was not with us."

"Is that why you left?"

"Fatima was tired. Diabetes. 'Only one place can protect us,' she said. 'Together, we will find God's garden.'" I cover a small yawn.

"I understand. We've had a long day." Yet Serafim makes no move to leave. Stretching my back, I lean against the window frame. Serafim is up and takes a few steps closer. I do not put my eyeglasses on—the shape of him allows me to imagine Zeca in his place. I feel faint, and when I open my eyes Serafim is by my side, holding my hand and my elbow to steady me. The ocean breezes are still.

"Every morning, with the call to prayer, Fatima and I walked to her fancy goods shop. She sat on her high stool behind her shop counter and read the newspaper in the morning, awaiting her first customers. I organized the colourful khangas and kitenges into their piles. Along one side of the shop were shelves displaying carvings, baskets, and gently used books. Below the shelves was a board covered in soft black fabric. Small pins held beautiful jewellery from tribes across Africa. She told me that nothing she sold there compared with the beauty of my mother's necklaces and earrings.

I cleaned the house for Fatima and minded the shop. She liked to send me to the market or to other vendors with notes, but she encouraged me to use my words. Lunch was always from KT Shop because she was friendly with the owner, who made *real* kabobs. Along its narrow roads, the city was always filled with market-goers. Radios droned, truck engines coughed and sputtered."

"And you felt safe by yourself? You were never lost?" Serafim stood close enough now that his breath warmed my neck.

"If I kept my eye on the grey-spired cathedral that was by the harbour, I knew where to turn and how to find my way back."

"How did people react to you?"

"As I said, the streets were packed with many kinds of people. They looked at me, but they were far too busy to stare. This was the big city and I could easily disappear there. I was a chameleon."

"Then why did you leave?"

"I wanted to stay. I learned Portuguese and a few words in English, a little Swahili. People did not mind me. Shop owners smiled and offered me blessings. They would call out to me, 'Pó,' and I liked the sound—the way my name lifted through the air."

"But why did you leave?"

I hear Amalia whistling before I see her skipping into the room. When she sees Serafim she freezes. I twist my body towards her and lose my balance and my knees buckle.

Serafim catches me before I hit the floor. "Amalia, pull back the covers. I need to get Pó into bed."

Amalia rushes at us, her face coming into focus. She kicks Serafim in the shin and wedges her body between us as Serafim stumbles back. Amalia guides me to the edge of my bed. I search for my eyeglasses on my head and lower them onto the bridge of my nose. I look to Serafim gathering his notebooks and pencils, his recorder and bag. He stuffs everything inside his satchel and swings it over his head and onto his shoulder.

"She is a fine protector. I can see you are in good hands," he says, raising his hand to wish us a good day.

"Filha, you can't do that to my friend."

Amalia removes the boots from my feet. My voice is caving in, losing most of its conviction. She senses it and throws her arms around my neck to hug me. Her fingers scolding open wounds. I fall back onto my pillow. I manage to turn onto my stomach, my cheek pressing into the pillow. The cancer is eating away at me. There is a constant burning weakness in my bones; the morsels of food I eat taste like metal. Every morning is a gift, but as the day passes I am reminded of precious time.

When I open my eyes, Amalia is holding a ripe mango and some rice in a tin. She peels the mango and with her juice-covered fingers places a small piece of the fruit between my lips.

Serafim

❋

THE DECISION WAS MADE in an instant. A visit from Fatima's friend Graça De Melo and her only daughter, Celestina, forced us to leave.

It was Christmas Eve. Fatima sat at the kitchen table across from Graça. Her daughter sat on the long bench against the wall. The table was covered with small dishes of treats: dates, lupino beans, figs, cashews, and small dishes of salted fish and berries.

When I served them tea, Senhora De Melo's body turned away. I stood close by, ready to fill their cups. They would not look at me.

"There is no other way to say this, but there is much talk in the city," Senhora De Melo said.

"There always is." Fatima smiled. "I have been here long enough to weather a monsoon or two, remember."

"They say . . ."

Celestina rose from the bench. "What my mother is trying to say." She kept crumpling a handkerchief, passing it from one hand to the other. "There are many people, shop owners, and others from rural areas, who are looking for people like her."

"Like Pó?"

"Surely you have heard, Fatima."

"What do they want from Pó?"

"She is an . . ."

I can still see Fatima's eyebrows far up her forehead, so high they brushed her head wrap. "She is a child of God. People will do almost anything to change their fortunes. They visit their healers and ask them for spells and charms."

"What does that have to do with Pó?" Fatima asked.

Celestina said, "There are some who believe albinos bring good luck, even wealth."

I had caught whispers amongst customers, had heard a group of soldiers shout the word from across the street, but had never attached the word to me—*albino*. I hadn't known what to call myself. I remember repeating the word in my head, to get used to the sound of it.

"There are many out there, and their numbers are growing,

who believe albino medicine is lucky." Senhora De Melo spat the words like watermelon seeds.

"You think I have not heard all these stories before?" Fatima kept twisting a corner of her sari. "I have heard there are many albinos in the Lake District. They kill them, butcher them. They believe that if you bury the limbs of an albino at the entrance of a gold mine, that mine will produce great wealth. Or if you tie an albino's hair into your nets you'll always catch a fish. The hands and skin are for luck in business. I know. I am a businesswoman. But these are silly stories." The end of her sari was now a ball in her fist.

I tried to pretend that I could not feel their eyes on me.

"I thought you might help," Celestina said.

"What is it you want?"

"Senhora Fatima," Celestina began. "Please. I have been married for five years, and for those years my husband waits patiently, but I cannot hold a child to term. I have seen every doctor and I have gone outside of the city. There are men that the natives trust and believe. I was— We were hoping that Pó might be willing to offer us some of her hair."

I reached up to cover my head. All the women turned to me now.

"You are one of my dearest friends, Fatima. All I ask is a bit of its hair and—"

"It! Her name is Pó," Fatima said, getting up from the table. "And you are not welcome here."

The door closed behind them.

Fatima lit a cigarette, sat quietly in her chair looking out her window. "We must get you out of here," she finally said, covering my hand with hers.

"I do not want to leave. Where will I go?" The idea of being pushed away again made it hard for me to swallow.

"We'll go to the mountain that God set upon the earth for his animals and his children," she said, sounding like her priest.

We. I would not be alone.

✳

I press Stop. I remove my earbuds and begin to jot down my notes. I scan the restaurant. It is still too early for people to gather. A few men sit at a table playing cards, smoking. A young woman sits alone, sipping on a drink, one long leg crossed over the other. She catches me looking at her and smiles. I look down to write.

NOTES: Sunday, Oct. 16, 2016. Restaurante Kanimambo
— Seemed preoccupied. ~~Not looking well.~~ Ophelia staying
  out all night. Pó fears for the girl's safety.
— Clear signs Pó is growing frailer each day. Her mind
  wanders or she forgets, not quite sure. Struggles to get
  up from bed. Speech often slurred or turns to an inaudible
  whisper.

— Steps/breathing have slowed. Looks tired—exhausted.
Actually left her room to check up on children's schooling
downstairs. Admitted she hasn't done that in quite a while.

— A growing urgency for her to finish her story. Seems she
is compelled to do so, even when she feels unwell. I must
admit feeling anxious—selfish on my part—for her to tell
me everything she has gone through.

— Brought her some lotion. Not sure it will help to soothe
pain from lesions around neck and shoulders. Skin
CANCER likely. What stage? Spread to lymph nodes?
[most likely] Red/purple patches ulcerating. Very
self-conscious. Covers up. I look away.

— Clear that educating albino children very important to
her. She sees this as key to successful futures—learning to
navigate their world with confidence. Education = survival.
Perhaps why recording her story is imperative; something
to leave behind.

— ~~Continues to~~ Also believes play is important—social
integration. Was an outsider herself and doesn't want these
children to be confronted with same barriers.

— Caught! Conflicting ideas, though. Essentially TRAPPED—
Wants them to connect to a bigger world but fears for their
well-being. Concerned they will be taken and killed. VERY
REAL concern in current political climate.

— In Tanzania, some 75 PWAs were reported killed between
2000 and 2016. There are MORE since many cases go

unreported, i.e., Fathers and mothers often urged to get rid of their infant, afraid their child with supernatural powers will bring misfortune to the family.

— Amnesty International: Albino body parts bring wealth, power or sexual conquest, and that having sex with a person living with albinism cures HIV and AIDS. Attackers sell albino body parts to ~~witch doctors~~ healers for thousands of dollars.

— Threats to albinos' lives are compounded by exclusion, stigmatization. Some are denied the basic right to an education and health.

— Time is a concern. May not have long. Pó's story will go unfinished?

I sense someone hovering over my shoulder. I lower my pencil, thinking my order of spicy prawns has arrived.

"Are you alone?" A quick scan and the table where the young woman had been sitting is empty. I look over my shoulder to see her standing close, her head bent toward me.

"I am," I say, covering my notes with my forearms—a gut instinct.

"Would you like company?" Before she hears my reply, she slinks into the chair. "Rosalia," she says. Her synthetic hair is straight and long, pulled back from her face. Her eyelids are an unreal blue, like peacock feathers, the backdrop to fake eyelashes that resemble large spiders.

"Serafim," I say, raking my fingers through my hair. My tongue feels thick in my mouth. I look around the room in search of another beer from the server. I hear a low hum. The ceiling fans have been turned on. The wobbling lessens as the blades gain speed, the air lifting Rosalia's hair from behind her ears, blowing strands across her face. Some hair sticks to her lipstick. She brushes it aside.

"I've seen you here before," she says, in a voice belonging to someone who has smoked all her life. "Are you a professor?" She places a cigarette in her mouth and lets it sit there. I reach for my lighter and light it, light one for myself.

"Something like that. I'm a journalist."

"I like stories." She smiles, and her teeth are marbled in yellow. She closes her lips quickly. When she crosses her legs, her dress rides high up her thigh. Her flip-flops slap up against her heel, tapping air, her toes clenched. "I've seen you going in and out of your hotel. You alone?" She grabs her drink and presses the cold glass to her collarbone, rolls it up her neck. She closes her eyes. A bead of water runs down her neck.

"Yes," I say.

"You don't have to be."

I think how easy and comfortable it would be to take her back to my hotel room, to feel her skin against mine.

I'm about to respond when the waiter lowers my plate to the table—piri piri prawns on a bed of rice. Before the flies can land, and without invitation, Rosalia picks up a prawn with her fingers and tears its head from its body. Looking directly at me, she sucks the juice from the prawn's head.

"I'm used to being alone," I say as she pinches the legs of the prawn and takes apart its shell. I nudge the plate closer to her. "Please, help yourself."

"Is there anything I can do to help?" Rosalia looks like she has all the answers.

"Perhaps," I say. Pó has been worried about Ophelia. Beira is not a safe place to stay out all night, especially for someone with albinism. Now it's my turn to lean in and whisper. "I don't know this place very well." Her foot has stopped tapping. "Can you help me?"

"It's what I do best," she says.

"Good. Then perhaps you've seen a young albino girl here on the streets at night."

Rosalia drops her prawn onto the plate.

"Ophelia," I say.

"Odette," she replies, lifting the napkin to her lips.

"No, I'm asking about a girl who goes by Ophelia. Do you know her?"

"On the streets she calls herself Odette. Keeps things separate, safe. She's a pretty little thing," she adds, and drops the crumpled napkin.

"So you know her?"

"What I know is it's not safe for her out here," she says. Both her feet are now on the floor. She presses down on the tabletop, about to get up.

I reach into my pocket and slip a couple of thousand meticais—thirty U.S. dollars—into her hand, more than she would have expected if I'd engaged with her in my room. "Watch over her," I say. She looks at me in a very different way now. "You know where I'm staying."

Ezequiel

THE PORTUGUESE REFER to Mozambique, and colonies like it, as *Terras do Fim do Mundo*. Driving north from Sofala through the province of Cabo Delgado—a thin coastal strip in the north where political control remains in colonial hands—it does feel like we've reached the end of the world. Except for me, who sees this place as a return. It is less than an hour's drive to the mission. I could go back.

Most villages we drive through are shantytowns—the shed skins of snakes. People are left with nothing except promises. The Portuguese, in exchange for loyalty and continued servitude, promise safety and security. FRELIMO offers freedom, and the almost impossible dream: the right to decide their own futures, to determine their own happiness.

"I don't want to visit the mission," I say, after the Commander presses me.

He remains quiet in the passenger seat beside me, his hands on his knees. At one point the road plunges steeply toward a river and a ramshackle wooden bridge. He rolls the window down to look at a group of children swimming in the green water, and the kneeling women washing clothes. I'm afraid he'll say something, or worse, ask me to stop so that he can stalk the women and children until they gather their things and run into the jungle.

"You're certain you don't want to return to the place you were raised?"

I can feel the motionless heat press on me. I roll my window down.

"Because that door will always stand open in your mind. A glimpse into your past might cure what troubles you."

"I can't go back." *Just one step in front of the next.*

I can feel his yellow eyes on me, trying to determine what I am made of.

"Good. In this continent, to revisit the past is to learn that God and the Devil are one."

It is late October and the promise of a long rainy season looms large. After a year of working by the Commander's side I have become the perfect shadow he wants. I have seen the debris of his madness—at least three girls that I know of, butchered by his hands. I thought of their mothers and fathers, their siblings, not knowing whether their daughters ran away or were taken from them, as I disposed of their bodies.

I trust no one. Being alone with my judgments makes survival easier, since I don't have to look out for anyone but me. I never felt comfortable leaving the Commander with girls, but often I never saw them enter his tent or room. Abel was in charge of procuring the young women. I would only find them the morning after, helpless in my inability to stop his madness. The truth is, even if I could, I wouldn't be able to do anything. At least that's what I tell myself. Commander Fonseca makes efforts to show kindness—setting me up in my own hotel room, giving me a few hundred escudos each week, leftover food and wine.

I make my way down to the lobby. People are chatting on the sofas. The hotel has been divided, refurbished to accommodate those in the military with titles: colonels, lieutenant colonels, majors, always in full uniform with shiny decorations. The hotel houses them and their families. The children are only allowed to play on the rooftop terrace, which overlooks Porto Amélia's harbour and the Indian Ocean. The staff extends sheets across posts and antennae to create some relief from the blistering sun. Mothers stand by the railing, drinking tropical concoctions and smoking. They never leave and they do not discuss the one thing they all know—that the hotel had once been a brothel, and only recently repurposed for the war effort.

The lobby of the hotel with no name is wide and the light filters through the curtains. The windows are tall, constructed of small square panes filmed with dust. The chandelier is still the same as before the war, when businessmen came by large ship to claim crocodile suitcases and elephant tusks. They would stay at the hotel a few days before setting out to conduct their business up or down the coast. That is why there are claw-footed bathtubs in our rooms. The place smells of old mixed with a trace of cheap perfume. I am reminded of my birth mother.

Outside, the palm trees curve. The big sun is dull and looms over the ocean and the city. A black waiter dressed entirely in white carries a tray over to Commander Fonseca leaning against the jeep. The Commander picks up the pack of cigarettes and the waiter bows slightly before backing away.

The Commander is not dressed in his uniform. He wears cream-coloured pants and a linen shirt, open to display his dark patch of chest hair. His shirt is already soaked in perspiration, and through the shirt I can see his ribs and flat stomach. Nothing about his relaxed dress puts me at ease. If anything, he looks agitated.

"This place is filthy," he says to me, spitting into the sand. "This would be a good country to live in if it weren't for the blacks. Mondlane wants to be their father, but he doesn't see what his children are capable of." It's always the same rant.

"You drive," the Commander says, tossing the keys to me. "Abel has errands today." I never ask what the chores are and Abel, if he is within earshot of the Commander's racist rants, remains expressionless. Whenever the Commander spews his poison, I think of my own ancestry. Increasingly, his words have an impact on me, and I often feel guilty. I am overwhelmed by them but remain straight-faced. For most of my life I saw myself as white. I chose to ignore any references to my blackness. I learned things would be easier for me that way. I can no longer deny that side of me. I am not safe here and a threat is always present.

I make a slow turn away from the hotel and onto the beach road. A group of women wrapped in their colourful capulanas walk with baskets on their heads. They hear the jeep coming from behind them and form a line. Commander Fonseca taps me on the shoulder to slow down. The women are Makua. Their faces are covered in mussiro—the thick white paste I'm familiar with. Only the mussiro prepared for me by Mother Anke was laced with bleach, and there are days when I look in the mirror and notice a tinge of blue to my skin.

The women look straight ahead. They know better than to look inside the jeep. At the front of the line is a girl, no more than fifteen, I would guess. She does not wear mussiro, nor does she carry a basket on her head. Instead, she holds on to a rope, which is secured around the neck of a goat. The girl is trying hard not to look our way.

"Menina," Commander Fonseca calls out, before whistling to get her attention.

I see her sidelong glance. She is beautiful as she fights a smile. The Commander sticks his head out the window and opens his mouth to say something, but before he can, I shift the jeep into gear and it kicks in acceleration. He keeps looking at the reflection of the girl in the side mirror.

We drive along the dirt road. The ocean breeze is never far from our side. A film of salt dusts my cheek and makes it difficult to run my fingers through my hair.

"Do you know where we're going?" the Commander says.

I do not answer.

"I need to get away from that suffocating place. Nothing ever happens there." He lights another cigarette, blowing smoke through his nose like a bull.

After an hour's drive past deserted beaches on one side and, on the other, fields of mango spread across the sandy terrain like a forest, the Commander asks me to veer onto a narrow dirt road. At the end of the road there is a weathered shack of bamboo and behind it forest.

"This is it," the Commander says. "Perfect spot for some target practice." He opens the back of the jeep and unfurls a cowhide. There are five guns, all different types.

"Go ahead," he says, and picks up a shotgun for himself.

My hand hovers over the guns before it settles on a black revolver with a wooden handle, a Colt Python.

"We're hunting, not playing a game of Russian roulette."
Go for the Armalite seven sixty-two."

The Commander leads the way. He carries his gun over his shoulder, and I do the same. He keeps looking back as if assessing how I hold a gun, my comfort with its weight. Perhaps it is a bold taunt or challenge, to see if I will take aim at him. I have never revealed a thing to him, but every so often he says something that tells me he knows details about my life I have buried deep. I don't believe the lieutenant would have shared the information he learned from my fevered mumblings. It makes my ears itch when the Commander alludes to my family on the mission or the men who took me into the jungle. I cannot show my discomfort.

The Commander spots a strip of mud at the edge of the sea. A flock of flamingos stand in the shore's shallow water, their heads and necks tucked underneath their wings. But the flamingos are not the animals that dazzle the Commander. A little farther off there is a troop of vervet monkeys. They have come to the water's edge to wash their food, twirling fruit or some other meal in the water in quick motions.

The Commander prepares to cock his weapon without taking his eyes off the monkeys. He aims the barrel of the rifle toward the open ocean, then lowers it to the mud, before scanning his gun from left to right. I want to bury my face in my hands. The gun goes off. The shot vibrates in the air. I am surprised the flamingos do not take flight. We are close enough that I can see the chaos surrounding the monkey that has been hit. It twitches before lying still. The other monkeys screech and yell, jump up and down in frantic motions. One of the bigger monkeys is trying to drag the dead monkey away. The Commander fires again. The bigger monkey collapses over the first one. There is pandemonium, but the monkeys do not leave the side of their downed family members. The flamingos unfurl their necks and poke at the shallow water as if nothing has happened.

The loyalty of the monkeys overwhelms me.

"Your turn. Shoot," the Commander says.

Dread surges up my throat.

"Shoot!"

I pull the trigger and miss.

The Commander looks up to a shimmer of green slowly covering the sun.

"It's going to rain," I say.

"Not rain," the Commander says, holding out his hand. A locust falls from the sky and lands dead in his palm.

"What's happening?"

Exhausted locusts begin to drop all around us. Some still flutter from their dive and fall.

"Can you hear the noise they make?" the Commander says, with a renewed enthusiasm.

The air turns glass-bottle green, as does the sea. The cloud of locusts descends on us. They rain down and I feel somehow privileged to witness the event. It's a sign.

The flamingos engage in an eating frenzy. They pluck the juicy insects that bob on the surface of the water, mistaking the locusts for fish. The monkeys remain unimpressed, huddled over their dead, preening them as if for a funeral. One of the monkeys stands on watch, his masked head scanning the surroundings. The locusts fall all around its feet, but it does not pick them up to eat.

When we arrive back at the hotel, the Commander insists that I come to his room to turn down his bed. This strikes me as suspicious, since a hotel worker comes every night to do this. The Commander says it is our last night before we push off from the coast and into the heart of the battle, Mueda.

"That girl," he says, looking at me, daring me to pretend ignorance. I won't walk into his trap. "Find her."

I walk out to the beach and step into the water. Gusts of wind kick up the sand in swirls. My face is blasted with a million pinpricks of sand and I feel alive.

It is past midnight. More than enough time to make the Commander believe I have scoured the city. I knock lightly on the Commander's door.

"Come in."

The room is dark, except for light from a single candle. Commander Fonseca is sitting in a chair. A shadow blacks out half of his face. There is enough light that I see a glass filled with drink and the revolver resting on his lap.

"I could not find her, Commander."

He shakes his head.

"I asked around. Spoke to everyone, and no one knows this girl. Perhaps she is not from these parts," I say, hoping he is too drunk to catch the tremble in my voice.

"Beatriz," he says. He holds up a hand to stop me. "Her name is Beatriz." He lifts the revolver and waves it toward the bathroom door. I open the door. The girl is hog-tied in the bathtub. Her face is plastered with mussiro; her tears have wet the area under her eyes. She is gagged and rests her forehead in exhaustion against the rim of the bathtub.

"I sent Abel out to find her for me. I knew you wouldn't do it." He clicks his tongue as though I'm a child who has misbehaved.

I step back into the room and there is nothing I can say. I take a step back toward the wall and lean against it.

The Commander directs me to the bamboo shack where earlier that day we spent hours taking refuge from the plague of locusts. The wind is strong, and with every gust the shack rattles. Shards of glass and splinters of wood cover the floor. A few rags and clothing are tossed on top of the stained mattress in the corner. Apart from the wooden table, two chairs, and a lantern at the edge of the table, the room is bare.

I am tied into one of the chairs. Abel drags Beatriz inside. He ties her torso to the back of the chair, the same way I have been tied. Our arms and hands are free. One of my eyes is shut and will not open. My head throbs and I take hold of it. I am beaten and too dazed to understand the wisdom of this.

Commander Fonseca is drenched.

"Abel, wait for me in the car."

Every breath I take is met with a sharp pain across my chest. I shiver, suddenly cold. The smell of pine cuts my nostrils and I remember the forest just behind the shack. With my one good eye, I take a clear look at Beatriz. It is clear she has been drugged. Her eyelids are heavy and her head hangs down and to the side, her chin touching her collarbone.

The Commander stands at the table. The six-chamber cylinder swings out to the left and he loads one bullet before spinning it to a click. He slams the revolver onto the table. "One of you will disappear tonight, become a ghost. I think it's only fair to let fate decide that."

I look at the gun and stare at what remains of this world. I feel defenceless, and the thought that I could grab the gun and fire at the Commander is futile.

"Spin it," he tells me through clenched teeth.

I spin the cylinder and press the gun to my temple. With my eyes closed I try to conjure Papa Gilberto. I want it all to be over. I want to run over the canopy of trees and reach the sun before it drops on the other side. I press down on the trigger. Click! I exhale and return the gun to the table.

Commander Fonseca slides the gun over to Beatriz. She is not quite sure what she is supposed to do. The Commander curls her fingers around the handle. While she holds it, he grabs her other hand and forces her to spin the cylinder. She can barely lift it to her head. The Commander wedges her mouth open and lets the gun barrel rest between her lips. I hear the clicking of her teeth against the revolver. She heaves, then clicks the trigger. She tries to stand up but she is firmly tied to the chair.

I take the revolver and for the second time I spin the cylinder. I raise it to my temple. I hold it firm and look directly at Commander Fonseca. I pull the trigger.

The Commander takes a long drag from his cigarette, holds his breath. He flicks the butt across the room, takes one step forward and the back of his hand strikes my cheek.

The revolver is in the girl's hand.

"Give it here! I'll go again." My voice cracks.

Beatriz spins the cylinder and places the gun upside down in her mouth, its black metal brutal against her delicate face.

"Give it to me!" I yell.

She holds the wooden handle of the revolver with both her hands to steady it. She uses her thumbs to ready the gun. She closes her cracked lips around its barrel.

❊

A sudden pop is followed by the tinny sound of metal expanding. The furnace kicks in. Warm air from the vent blows into my bedroom.

The door is still locked.

After I let the furnace man into my apartment, I closed myself off in my room and got under the covers. I want to stay here till the repairman leaves. I'll let the heat fill my room and remain inside until dark.

"Sir?" He's knocking. "I'm leaving now. The furnace is running fine."

"Thank you."

"I left my number tagged on the furnace. If you have any questions, call and ask for Eduardo."

His name speeds through my brain and I cannot stop it. *Eduardo. Eduardo. Eduardo.* Monday, February 3, 1969, and everything changed.

❋

Lately, a persistent call has been waking me early each morning.

Propping myself up in bed, I free my legs from the hotel sheets and run my hands lightly over my blistered feet. Ten thousand miles, maybe more, mining track in the bush of northern Mozambique, and hundreds of innocent people, women and children among them, all gone because of me. I need to break free, make amends. The Commander says I must do this one more thing for him. He saved me, he said, so I could atone for my disloyalty.

With one hand I change the direction of the antenna and use my other hand to turn the dial on the transistor radio on my nightstand. The signal from Mozambique is strong enough and a voice crackles through the tiny speaker. A commentator mocks FRELIMO. The guerrillas are resisting colonial rule. They demand a role in a new government. But the man tells his listeners FRELIMO can't have a voice in shaping Mozambique's future because they simply don't understand how to run a country. He is speaking of the country I am in now, Tanzania. He says the Africans there have grasped nothing, learned nothing. When the British flag was struck down and they raised their own, it was the beginning of a funeral procession. The man reassures his listeners that an increased military presence in the northern provinces has begun and soon all will be secured.

I roll my shoulders and slap my thighs awake. I yawn, stand up to stretch, naked, staring up at the ceiling. A water stain travels down one corner. I step into a rectangle of light on the floor and catch my reflection in the full-length mirror. My eyes are dark. I try to arrange the straggling wisps of hair that stick to my forehead. The mirror makes me look tall, even though I am of medium height, but I am pleased with what I see, toned and lean. My skin is darker. I need to shave. All attempts to grow a beard have failed. There is a patch of hair on my chest that trails down to my pubic area. I touch my cock.

I feel powerless as I look down at the reflection of my hands; at the ink the Commander cut into me—five dots between my thumb and forefinger. I will not let him possess me again. I am hungry and at war, but after today, everything will change.

The streets of Dar es Salaam are coming alive. Vendors set up their wares: bolts of fabric, pails, sandals dangling from hooks, small bags of teas and coffee beans, piles of folded khangas, their colours bleeding into each other. There are scarves, kofias stacked high, twine, locks, chains, washboards. Some of the vendors sit to smoke and drink strong coffee. Soon, they will all be shouting over each other.

I dodge the traffic—broken-down taxis and dubious dala dala buses mix with bicycles and wooden toroli carts all honking for a way out. Dar es Salaam is far more energetic than Porto Amélia. I've been scoping the city for a few weeks, going over my planned route, timing everything. In all this time I haven't adjusted to the early-morning stench of sewage wafting from the gutters or along the roads where water and urine and blood from the butcher shop sit stagnant at the curb.

I turn around quickly. I do not see Abel. The Commander sent him here to ensure I carry out my orders properly. Abel has become my shadow. I am certain that once this task is completed, I will be killed.

I reach the unmarked storefront. As planned, no words are exchanged. A hard-boiled egg and a pot of spiced coffee are brought to my table. I manage a few sips of coffee before the waiter returns with a parcel.

"Do not stop. Do not speak to anyone."

The recipient's name is written clearly, Mr. Eduardo Chivambo Mondlane, the leader of FRELIMO. PIDE has gone to great pains to make the parcel appear as if it has been posted from the Netherlands. The combined counter-intelligence of two states has devised a simple letter bomb wrapped like a book. If asked about the contents upon delivery, I've been instructed to simply drop the package.

"And run?" I had asked the Commander.

"No need," he replied. I did not allow him the satisfaction of seeing my fear, the flush of panic, and the way the muscles in my face ticced underneath my skin.

Leaving the shop, I hold the parcel in both hands and think of Eduardo Mondlane, the soft-spoken intellectual. They say he abandoned his texts for war. A true freedom fighter.

A black car is parked in the small square. Whoever is inside has a clear view of the storefront I have just exited. I cannot see the driver, but I know it is Abel. I turn the corner and lose my footing on the curb that has crumbled away. *One step becomes a hundred. Just one step in front of the other.* I tuck the parcel in my satchel.

I shift the carrier bag so that it rests flat on my lower back. I can feel the parcel through the bag's thick canvas. I straddle my motorbike and turn on the ignition. The ride is not bumpy. I have mapped out every divot and every portion of unpaved coastal road. I pass the railway station and the ferries that shuttle people across to Zanzibar. I lean forward and shift gears, allowing my chest to vibrate in tandem with the engine. In my rear-view mirror, I can see the black car tagging along. I breathe in the clean ocean air mixed with the pungent scent of eucalyptus from cook fires. These are the smells that waft through family homes and outside camps. I push the thought out of my mind.

With my sweaty palms gripping the handles, I ride for twenty minutes until I begin to see the large homes and manicured gardens of Oyster Bay, a very different Dar es Salaam. The houses are a brilliant white, surrounded by high fences and barbed wire. There are uniformed guards and armed police-men on watch. A group of men with machetes on their belts and hedge clippers in their hands loiter by the guards.

I stop behind a bus in front of Mondlane's home. The gates are open and a guard stands by the door. The car is not in the driveway, which means Mondlane has left for his office. He is following his routine. I had to be certain.

It is still early when I get back to the city. I stand across from the building where the FRELIMO offices are located. There are police officers in front. I do not cross the square. Instead, I walk along the storefronts and office buildings. As I approach, a cou-ple of police officers notice me reaching for the parcel in my bag. They stop their talk. Their hands go to their guns. *Relax. Breathe.* It's not wise to look these men in the eye. I look down at the parcel, the intended's name so clear. The FRELIMO office is too noisy and crowded. Mondlane goes in every morning but only to pick up his mail. I walk up to the entrance where a uniformed man sits at a desk. The police officers resume their discussion.

"I have a package," I say, raising it up to my chest and tilting it slightly. "Mr. Mondlane?" I say, reading the label as if I'm uncertain of the name.

The guard at the desk shells pistachios and pops them into his mouth. He looks at the officers. They are indifferent. He motions me closer. He stands up, reaches for his rifle and taps its muzzle on top of the package.

"For Mr. Mondlane?" he says, in Kiswahili.

"It's a special delivery from the bookshop on Samora." Although I could communicate, I practised the words in Kis- wahili until there was no trace of a Portuguese inflection.

The guard drinks his beer and upends his glass. A mous- tache of foam remains on his lip. He wipes his mouth with the back of his hand. "I'll take it," he says.

The door swings open and a tall man walks out. I know it is Eduardo Mondlane from all the photos and newspaper clip- pings. I didn't think he'd be such an imposing figure close up.

"A package for you, sir," the guard says, standing up to block his glass of beer from Mr. Mondlane's sight.

I hold the package in my hands. Mr. Mondlane's eyes lock with mine and I see the kindness and intelligence of this man.

"For me?" he says, reaching for the parcel.

I hold on tighter than I thought. Once it is firmly in his grasp,

I can do nothing but look at the coin he has placed in my palm. He brushes by me, his mail and the package tucked under his arm. He slips into a waiting car. As he does every morning, he will make his way to Betty King's house. She is an American lady who works for the African-American Institute, an NGO sympathetic to the cause of independence. An informant has told me that she has given him a corner office in her home—a place to reflect and meditate and discuss important issues with his comrades.

I turn to leave. I see Abel across the square. He has surely witnessed the exchange. Closing his car door, he begins to cross the square. I slink behind a slowly passing truck and walk with it, blocking Abel's view. I fight the urge to run. I need to stay hidden and get lost in the crowd. As the truck pulls away I drop and roll under a parked car. I do not want to look back, but I must. When I do I see Abel, searching the busy square. I slip out from under the car and dart into a side street. For an instant my mind goes blank and I'm afraid I've lost my bearings, until I see the motorcycle I have stowed at the entrance to a building.

I jump on my motorcycle and begin to weave through the narrow alleys and streets. Abel's car cannot follow me at the same speed, but he will soon figure out where I have gone. I cannot stay long, and I'm not certain why I am drawn to King's house—my role is done.

I ride slowly by the house and see that Mondlane's car is parked in the driveway. His driver and a guard lean against the car, smoking.

It is a clear day, and looking over the glittering ocean I catch a glimpse of Zanzibar's coastline. The dhows skim the sea's surface. These are the same boats that have sailed these waters, unchanged, for centuries.

It happens in an instant—the heat of the explosion hits me and I'm thrown to the ground. I hear yelling and the scraping of metal against concrete, the sound of a car horn that will not stop.

From close by I hear a rifle's quick snap. In a daze I see men from neighbouring homes raise their guns, shaking themselves into motion, running toward the little house by the sea. It is all unravelling in horn-filled slow motion. I manage to get up on one knee. A corner section of the house is hollowed out like the bite of an apple. The billowing white smoke turns grey.

Perhaps the war is over now. Everything will go back to the way it was. Cashews will drop into my palms. Papa Gilberto will appear from the mountains unharmed.

The dust has a familiar smell—a whiff of iron, like the scent of dried blood. My ears ring to the sound of the sea: "Run, Ezequiel. You are free."

2.
In God's Garden

Ezequiel

HEAVY RAIN HAS STRIPPED the oak tree in the front yard of its last leaves and the wind has funnelled them into the walkway I share with my neighbour. I know he will be upset. It's my tree. I should rake the leaves up before the snow falls.

A child's cry, the same wailing that kept me up through the night, starts again. The renters upstairs have brought home another child. I haven't seen the couple for months and didn't know she was pregnant.

❋

There is nothing we can do to make Mother Anke feel better about our lives in the mission. Every day she pleads with Papa to leave.

"Anke, please. We're going around in circles with this. It's nonsense," he tells her.

Outside Papa's office door, I slide down to sit on the floor and press my back against the wall.

"You are away so often. You don't see it, Gilberto." She has to pause to catch her breath. Portuguese is not her language of anger. She told me she met Papa when she was eighteen. Her parents were Dutch missionaries looking to set up a mission in Mozambique. They didn't last but Mother Anke stayed with Papa.

"The planes are getting louder. I place my head on the pillow and hear land mines exploding in the distance."

"Anke! It's your imagination playing tricks."

"I can smell the sulphur, Gilberto."

"You're tired. We're all tired," Papa says, "but this will pass. This is our home."

"They will take everything we have. They hate us for our skill, our ability to organize, the way we make things work."

"Soon you'll say they hate us most because their magic doesn't work on us. So we allow terrible men to lead us, defend our right to make money off their sweat, their blood."

"You always take their side."

I can hear the defeat in her words.

"No. I simply don't believe that the blacks are whetting their knives to slit our throats while we sleep."

"The Liberation Front is gaining momentum. There will be a war."

"What would you have me do?" Papa says. "Our workers take refuge here."

"You talk as if we cannot be touched. You have the boy believing it too. He sees a helicopter and thinks it is a toy. All the Portuguese can do is dig land mines in the thousands, and the only ones hurt are the farmers and their children who step on them. Can't you smell the fires burning?"

"Our flock is loyal to God and to us."

"And your loyalty to me? You promised me if I did not feel safe here we would return to the Netherlands, back to my parents' home."

"This is our home. This is my home, and I will protect what we have built," Papa says, his voice tired and cracking.

"They will turn, but then it will be too late."

She locks herself in her bedroom. I slip into Papa Gilberto's office to take my spot on the rug in front of his big desk. The night is filled with sounds, with insects and frogs and the low murmurings of cattle. These sounds are familiar and yet every night I'm surprised by how close they are.

Papa Gilberto sets aside his work and pours himself a glass of port. He places his new record on the turntable. I like the scratching and popping sounds of the record player, when the needle hits the record and skips, almost as much as the music itself. Papa has tried to explain how the needle works on the record album. I'm only interested that its tip is made of diamond. There is one song that begins like a stutter, as if the needle is caught in the record's groove. Then the song builds and rises; it makes me feel like I have climbed a mountain and am looking down as only a bird can. I wonder how something so beautiful could come from something that sounds gloomy, as if the woman singing is lost and can't find her way back. Papa's feet poke out from underneath his desk. His shoes are worn and crinkled. He lets me buff his shoes every day, and when I do I like to add up all the things that have contributed to them looking so old. Time plus dirt plus bends, so that the creases in the leather are just so.

The song ends. Papa lifts the arm back to the beginning. When we've listened to the song at least ten times, he cranks the record player once more and lets the rest of the album play out. He lies on his back beside me. He is large and warm. He clasps his hands behind his head. I copy. I am part of him and he's part of me.

"That song is beautiful," I say.

"I'm glad you think so."

"Is the woman sad?"

"I'm not certain, filho. It's in German," he says. I can't see his face.

Why can't I see his face?

"Papa!"

❊

The panic jolts me from my dream. I kick the sheets off and look around the room.

As I sit on the couch the basement door opens. I hold my breath. A large woman walks in, her hospital shoes so quiet she appears to float.

"How you feeling today?" she says, dropping her closed umbrella and purse on the La-Z-Boy.

I stare at her as she bends down to place slippers on my feet. "These floors are too cold. You'll get sick." The little light that comes through the window stretches her shadow as she goes to the refrigerator and unsticks a note. She stands in front of me, the note held a foot away from my face—HELEN, scrawled in thick marker.

Helen takes a sip from a paper cup. I close my eyes and breathe in her coffee breath. She moves around the apartment, shutting cabinets, clanging pots, wiping counters.

A wave of loneliness fills me; my guts turn inside out. But Helen's calm voice and the way she places her purse on her lap as she sits in the chair reassure me.

"Sure is getting chilly out there." She smiles. Perfect teeth. "I brought you a book. It's *exotic*," she says, like it's a dirty secret. I want to sleep. "It takes place in the jungle. Thought you'd like me to read some of it to you." She wiggles into the chair like a hen in its nest. "It might bring back memories of home."

I'm fearful of what my long ramblings, fits of disappointment, sparks of excitement might have revealed.

"They're in the jungle, you see, and this man is pulling a piece of rope attached to a trolley which his wife is standing on."

My cheek twitches.

"Imagine that!" Her eyes wide. "Crazy as loons, I know. But I can't put it down."

This woman sitting in front of me does not know my pain, the anxiety that digs its nails into me every day. She cradles two pills in her outstretched hand. I open my mouth, stick my tongue out like an eager boy taking communion.

I try to think of when a visitor sat there last. Three or four different nurses rotate throughout the week but there have been no visitors. Helen's reading glasses rest on the end of her nose. I turn away to look out the rain-slicked window. The wind has kicked more leaves into a small heap that blocks precious autumn light.

"What I am about to tell," she begins, and there is nothing I can do to stop her. I brace myself for the welcome burn of my medication. I want to return to Mount Gorongosa with a feeling of calm. I'm not certain what will soon play out in my head. Is it something I experienced or simply recreated? I don't think I'll ever understand.

My eyes close just enough that I can see my lashes webbing the light.

"Pó drinks the rain," I whisper.

I can't swallow. I gasp, struggling with the rights words.

Helen grabs hold of my hand and squeezes. "We will be giants once again."

❉

I ran for nine months, with nothing more in mind than to create distance between myself and the Commander. I kept safely away from the sporadic homesteads and ruined farmhouses that dotted the landscape. A few times I dared onto fields, ready to eat whatever I could find. If I was lucky I'd catch a guinea fowl or trap a rabbit.

I sailed along the shoreline on unsuspecting ships, from island to island, and when it was time to come ashore, I thought only of how far I had come, how much farther I needed to go. Sleep was not my companion. It eluded me as it had for years.

In the blueness of a November morning, I enter a stretch of fever tree blossoms as bright as their trunks. Only when I come through their shade do I see a mountain rising into mist.

A cane rat appears from behind a panga panga tree. It stops in the middle of the path and looks straight at me before scurrying up the slope. I follow.

The forest is cool. I walk on a carpet of flowering balsam plants and bamboo grass. The songs of the forest birds, some of which I have never heard before, echo in the wind. Everything on the mountain appears contained, kept from the rest of the world, as if under a glass dome. For the first time in months, perhaps in years, I feel joy.

I lean over the pool. The water moistens my lips, my chin, the cool rush of water running down my throat. I want to giggle like the boy I once was.

I curl into myself, let the birdsong drown out the sound of gunfire, always present in my mind. I catch a glimpse of scuffed boots that have snuck up beside me. They are the boots of a soldier, their toes sinking into the mud by the pond's bank.

I close my eyes and draw in a deep breath. It's all over.

A cloth brushes against my cheek. I remain still. A sheet is draped over a pair of bare legs, cinched at the waist. I see the face of a woman standing over me.

"Pó," she says, the word like a puff of smoke.

She moves away when I stir. I want her to stay close.

She does not take her eyes off me. I remain quiet, careful not to move and frighten her. She is not my captor.

She climbs over mosses and ferns, never once slipping. She calls from somewhere deep in the forest, "Follow me."

I navigate the steep hillside and clamber over a rock ledge. I climb up onto a jungle plateau halfway up from the foothills. Pó sits on a fallen log, waiting for me. She wears red sheets wrapped around her body, one over each shoulder. I have seen young Maasai men dressed like this, but never a woman. An albino. Pó crosses her leg over one knee and unlaces one boot, then the other.

"My name is Ezequiel," I say, undoing my boots too. "What do you call this place?"

She ties her laces together and tosses the boots over her shoulder, raises the water jug to her head and stands. "Only men need names," she says in rough Portuguese. She turns away to climb a steeper part of the mountain where a narrow, worn path of earth cuts along the slope. It is second nature to her. I struggle, hoisting myself up by grabbing the fronds of giant plants.

We arrive at a pristine pool fed by a waterfall a hundred or more feet high. A small group of warthogs are drinking by the water's edge. They scurry away, as do the monkeys and baboons.

Pó lowers the water jug from her head to kneel on a large stone by the falls. She reaches down to splash water on her face and neck. Her skin is pale and paper-thin. Her nose and cheeks are crowded with freckles, the only marks on her translucent complexion.

She continues up the steep ascent until it gives way to a gentler slope. We walk out of the jungle onto the granite of one of the lower massifs. I stand next to Pó and look out from the mountain's peak. The flood plains, dry and golden, spread across the horizon, teeming with movement.

"You are safe here," she says.

I drop my head to my chest, let the rifle I had bought from a merchant slip from my shoulder to the ground. I allow my breathing to slow.

When I open my eyes, Pó is standing in front of me. "The rains are coming," she says.

A dozen or so rondavels are arranged in a circle, the entrances of the mud huts facing a clearing in the middle. We move slowly, cutting between two huts, and enter the clearing. The women and children, who had been going about their business, stop. An older boy sucks in his breath as if a snatch of something was about to come out of his mouth. Some of the women secure their grips on their idle machetes. Some Ndau had worked at the mission. I recognize the jewellery one woman wears around her neck. The children gawk. Some are urged to enter the nearest hut, but they freeze and stare at me and the rifle strapped across my shoulder, almost sensing I am part of some bigger story.

I am disappointed that we are not alone.

"That is Machinga," Pó says, pointing. "Vasco, the stone grinder, is her husband."

The villagers who remain in the clearing veer from our path, waiting for me to pass with Pó. Some raise their machetes. An older woman, her crinkled hair piled high above her round face, does not move.

"Stay close," Pó says, taking my hand. "Machinga. This man will stay with me," she says. It is all I understand of her Portuguese dialect.

The woman says something in her own dialect that mixes

her nasal clicks with Portuguese. She refuses to look my way, stands proudly in her bare feet.

"Yes, he is a stranger, but he will not harm us," Pó says, releasing my hand. She looks toward the worn path. She is asking me to follow it.

Halfway up the path, I turn back and see the centre of the village, thick smoke rising from the fire. The villagers' curiosity is focused on the conversation between Pó and Machinga. Some of the women are huddled around the fire, carving up a small antelope carcass, and have resumed their song. Naked children take up play again with sticks and what looks like a ball, poking at it rolling in the dirt. They catch me watching and turn giddy. I can't imagine how I must look. They must think the war has brought me to their mountain. What do they know of men like me? How much contact have they had? Do I look different to them? I must represent uncertainty in their world, which in every other way knows only sameness. One woman draws her child to her side. Another woman lifts her infant and swings him to her hip before slipping into a hut. The rest remain in a state of cautious curiosity.

A very old man, the only man I see in the village, is bent over a grinding stone. He presses the tip of a spear to the rim of the stone, grinding the metal in a rhythmic sweep across its surface. Machetes and a few spears lean against the wall of the straw hut.

Pó catches me staring, and with a gentle wave of her wrist urges me to keep walking. She walks from the clearing and winds her way to meet me. I walk ahead. At the end of the path, set apart from the village, is a small mud hut.

"Has it been settled? Is it safe here?"

"Wait," she says, before lowering herself into the entrance and drawing the flap of skins behind her.

Sitting against a tree stump, I drift in and out of sleep. Every so often, the sun breaks through the cloud cover and beats down on me. I need water. I try to get up, move toward the jug Pó has set by the hut's entrance, but my knees buckle. I notice a child walking up the path, his arms outstretched. I use the tree stump to get up, stagger and fall. The child now stands above me. Some of the other children and a few women have wound their way up the path behind the boy, the same boy who had wanted to speak earlier. He bends down and stabs at something on the ground. I reach for my rifle but it is not there. I see it lying in the sand a few yards away. I hold up my hands. The boy skewers the ball the other children had been playing with, and only then do I realize it is an animal's eyeball, perhaps plucked from the butchered antelope.

"Kwazi," the boy says, pounding his chest.

"Zeca," I say.

Thunder roars in the distance. Kwazi looks up, surveys the sky. I dig into my pocket and draw the harmonica out. My hand cups and quivers to make the first note reverberate. Kwazi seems intrigued by the sound.

Pó emerges. I stop playing. Her arms are covered in wooden

bracelets, her head topped by an Englishwoman's hat. A massive collar of coloured beads and shells circles her neck and rests on her shoulders. Like everyone else, I remain silent.

As I slip the harmonica back into my pocket, Pó goes back into her hut and with some effort backs out with a rusted wheelchair, a strange object on a mountain. However it got here, its effect is instant. The crowd hurries down the path to take their places in the clearing. What I see next is even more surprising. Underneath a black umbrella secured with twine to the back of the chair sits a woman. She wears a lace veil over her head, but I can see her thick hair, grey-streaked and straight. I had seen many women like her in Tanzania, dressed in silks—turquoise and fuchsia—with tiny mirrors sewn around their hems. She sits proudly in her battered chair with armrests made of branches. Her toes poke out from underneath her tangle of saris. Her fingers flick the beads of her rosary. Pó pushes the woman down the path and into the middle of the village. They begin to circle the fire in the clearing. The woman cranes her neck from under the umbrella's brim to look up to the sky. One of the chair's wheels is crooked and with every turn makes the sound of a whining instrument.

Pó does not speak to the woman she is pushing. They both look up. At first, I think they are looking for the distant drone of warplanes and helicopters. I have grown sensitive to their droning. The sky rumbles and scythe clouds shift. Rain pours down in sheets of silver that disappear into the earth. Pó slips off her hat, and it rests on her back tethered to a string around her neck. She lifts her chin and opens her mouth to drink.

Everyone stretches out their arms and is drenched by the rain. My head stops throbbing. The noises from the children, the thanks from the women, Pó's laughter are silenced in my mind by the way the woman in the wheelchair studies me.

Pó

ONE LEG OF THE CHAIR is shorter than the other three. Rot or termites or both. Shifting my weight, I am able to balance. My body aches. The mosque is lit by a single floodlight on a pole high above its roof. From my balcony I see all the life around me. I see a mother tying her baby snuggly to her back. A teenager with a finger in his mouth leans against the Coca-Cola machine. The old man, Paolo, shuffles in his broken shoes and drags a bulging bag over rubble. There are others. They all cross the grounds and disappear into one or another of the hotel's blocks, like ants to their anthill.

Behind me, Serafim sits in his chair, which he has moved closer to the opening leading onto my balcony. He says when I am telling my story my voice grows quiet and drifts far away. His small recorder rests on the table next to him. He looks eager in his linens. When he leaves, his clothing will look like a damp rag that has been wrung, wrinkles across his back and thighs and where the top of his belly meets with his chest.

"It was raining the morning we left Dar es Salaam."

"Before you continue—sorry—can you tell me more about Fatima. How she got her reputation as a madwoman." Serafim's pencil hovers over his notebook.

"No one knew when Fatima had arrived in Dar es Salaam from Goa, or how old she'd been. No one could remember her ever being young. She smoked. It shocked the men who came to do business with her to see a woman roll her own cigarettes. Equals, she'd say. A smart businesswoman, but a terrible driver. She once borrowed a jeep and we drove up the coast at high speed with the top down. My stomach got boat sick, the way we veered from one side of the road to the other. My fingers got stiff from holding on so tight."

"You were sixteen when you left Dar?"

"Yes. Fatima wanted to protect me. From Graça and her daughter. And the war."

I remove my eyeglasses, rub the corners of my eyes. Pressing hard makes a wet sound in my head. Serafim becomes a blurry shape. One night, before we left Dar es Salaam, Fatima reached over to her night table and lifted a thin gold box to her lap. She opened it and showed me a small mirror. It was so close to my face that it was the first time I had seen myself clearly. I could see how the freckles were splashed across my nose, the apples of my cheeks. She lifted the small pink cushion from the box and patted my nose and cheeks. Small puffs of a powder lifted around my eyes. I took in the sweet smell and in the mirror I saw how the golden spots on my nose and cheeks had faded.

Pó, Fatima had said, dragging her forefinger down my cheek and neck. *It is Portuguese for dust or powder.*

Serafim crosses his legs. He settles in for a bit more information.

"Did you understand why Fatima felt so responsible for you? Why your mother knew Fatima could be trusted?" He lights another cigarette between yellowed fingers and leans back in his chair.

"When she was young, my mother used to visit Fatima. She and her family would come to the city after the rains, searching for green pastures to feed their cattle. Fatima and my mother were friends."

Part of me is aware that I'm giving Serafim what he wants. He is directing my story in a way that I'm beginning to resent.

I put on my eyeglasses. Serafim is back in focus. From the corner of my eye I catch a flash of colour. Ophelia is walking alongside the pool. With her dyed hair and a bright pink tracksuit, she keeps looking over her shoulder. She runs by the vegetable patch, a streak of hot pink, and turns the corner, disappearing around the small mosque in the direction of Beira's centre. The Coca-Cola machine's red light throbs across the vacant pool. There's nothing I can do to stop the girl from meeting with men on the beach or behind the bars. She wants to be a teenager—just one of them.

"We call it a beating heart," I say.

"What?"

"The Coca-Cola machine. It will die soon."

Serafim rises to stand next to me. His hands curl around the railing near mine. His arm brushes against mine and I swear I can feel every single hair. I close my eyes and take in a deep breath of his smell.

There is no breeze and the city is quiet. With Serafim by my side, I find the courage to continue—to feel we occupy the same moment in time, without time making a move.

✹

"It's a year since Ali Khamis Mohammed's ship brought us here. The people who live here call it God's Nest. The villagers who live at the bottom of the mountain refer to it as the place where the four rivers are born. We've made peace with the people here. I have been respectful of their ways and they have allowed us to remain. We know nothing of this man, and Machinga is concerned he will disrupt everything."

The first words from Fatima's mouth had been stewing in her belly when I wheeled her back into our hut the day Ezequiel arrived. Fatima was right. When we arrived, Fatima, being the businesswoman she was, recognized Machinga's stature in the village and gifted her a silk scarf and sari. Two blankets and a few of our metal pots were to be shared by the villagers. These offerings had been accepted, even though the women must have had misgivings. We did not look like them, but we did share enough words to understand each other. Machinga was married to Vasco, who had come from the bottom of the mountain. The Ndau often intermarried with the local population. They helped us build our shelter. She had become our sponsor, and Fatima shared her cooking spices with the villagers, tilled what land we could, side by side with them. Soon, I was asked to school the children, teach them the basics of language the way Fatima had taught me.

"Nothing good will come of this."

"We will see" were the only words I said to her that night.

Over the next week, with Kwazi's help, Ezequiel worked on a strong lean-to that could withstand the winds and the heavy rains. He remained quiet. Everything he did—the way he twisted his body to strike a post into the earth, his strong hands binding twine, his eyes turning bright when gathering supplies from Kwazi and his friends, rewarding the children with a song— all these things made me feel I was right to bring him back with me.

One night Ezequiel's music was replaced with the scritch-scratch of writing. I closed my eyes to the sound and drifted to sleep. During these quiet moments, I would ask Kwazi to deliver comforts to Ezequiel's shelter. A sleeping mat one day, an animal skin another. A candle so that he could write longer into the night.

I did not hear the drip-drip in the morning. Fatima snored when she slept on her back. She had been sleeping longer at night and often lay down to rest two or three times a day. Her legs could not carry her easily and she was not eating. Padre Theuns, a priest in Beira, had given us the wheelchair. He had also helped us secure passage to the foot of Gorongosa. At first, Fatima had refused, but after praying with her priest she allowed the man to load the chair on the back of a truck. Carrying Fatima up the mountain, strapped to her chair with vines, took three days with the help of some villagers. Fatima paid them well to get her to the top of Gorongosa.

When I stepped outside the next morning, an audience of six children sat waiting for me.

"*Bom dia*," I said, presenting them books from behind my back.

Ezequiel rolled out from underneath his shelter. The children giggled when they saw him. The hair on his head where he'd slept stuck up like the tail of a mating bird.

The look he had when I first found him lying by the pool on the side of the mountain—the hollowed-out face of a man lost in the world—had left him.

"A story!" one child cried.

"Yes! A story," Ezequiel said, echoing the excitement of the children.

Fatima had brought two books with us up the mountain: the Bible and Kipling's *The Jungle Book*, the book her father had given to her as a girl. Both books had been translated into Portuguese. I never read Kipling's book to the children. I only showed them the pictures of animals they recognized, elephants and snakes, and lions with zebra stripes, which Fatima called tigers.

❋

I stop. My voice is growing hoarse. I allow myself to remember how Ezequiel looked at me. He did not gape at me like the soldiers in Dar es Salaam. They would crouch against the wall in front of Fatima's shop, laughing and smoking. They tracked me with their eyes and whispers. I would shift and hide behind a pile of khangas. Here, I was exposed. Ezequiel did not turn away. I start again.

❋

The days passed. The rains continued to fall and the mountain grew greener.

Every day Ezequiel busied himself in the village. The tribesmen had been away hunting for a long time. When a few of them returned, some of the women reassured the men that Ezequiel meant no harm. Others would not talk to him or meet his gaze. They watched him constantly and wanted him to leave. His lean-to was once lit on fire. They did not trust Ezequiel. By the time the men set out again for another long journey, they allowed him to stay. They knew of a rifle's power, recognized that he could offer protection while they were away. The men decided he could stay for two months. When they returned, they would revisit their decision.

"Why must the men leave?" Ezequiel asked.

"They will not kill the animals on the mountain."

My answer did not satisfy Ezequiel.

"They fear the fighting will make its way up the mountain," I told him. "They are looking for another place to live." Then I asked about what had been worrying me. "Will you tell me about the fighting?"

"I don't know what to say."

"What happened to you?"

He shook his head. "I don't remember."

"You ran away?"

Ezequiel looked down at his hands. He considered me but could not find the words.

❋

I am aware that Serafim is still in the room. I allowed my thoughts to carry on ahead of me. Perhaps it was that first real exchange with Ezequiel that I wanted to keep all to myself.

✻

Ezequiel tried to reassure the women in the village. He dug for roots and picked berries with the women who allowed him to come near them. He stood by the blind man, Vasco, every day until the man gave in and taught him how to grind maize and sharpen machetes on the village stone. He stopped carrying his gun. He grew more comfortable with walking barefoot on the mountain.

I fed Fatima bits of food, whatever she could keep down, and she would fall asleep. When she began to snore, I would crawl out of our hut to stretch.

Ezequiel would build a small fire between his lean-to and our hut. He would sit on one of the two logs he had arranged around the stones he had lined for a pit. He'd scribble notes or play his harmonica. One night I found him there. He was bare-chested. His rifle leaned against the log next to him. He stopped twisting his hands and looked up.

"What do you have there?" I think I asked. I remember protecting my head from mosquitoes with one of Fatima's saris.

Ezequiel reached over the fire to show me a piece of wood. "I like to carve things. Animals, mostly. It passes the time."

"What will it be?"

He held the crude carving close to my face. He knew my eyesight was weak, but I didn't feel self-conscious. "I'm not sure yet. Soon its shape will tell me what it will become."

It seemed that every day it took Fatima longer to get up. She would lie in bed, tangled in her saris, rubbing her swollen legs to get the blood flowing. I used the ointment Machinga had made, rubbing it between my hands until they grew warm. I touched Fatima's feet. I knew the salve only numbed the pain. Fatima swore the pain disappeared, if only briefly, and she would sink back on her sleeping mat.

"I have something to show you," Fatima said one day. "I have only found it now, tucked in a book." She reached into the slip that covered her pillow. She offered me a fine leather booklet. I opened it. Fatima rolled over and handed me the magnifying glass. She said, "It's the only thing I have left of her."

It was a small black-and-white photograph of a much thinner and younger Fatima dressed in safari gear—a linen suit and a scarf wrapped around her head. She sat in an upholstered chair. Behind her stood a young black woman, strong and beautiful. The woman was dressed in a shuka. The pattern of her beaded necklace and earrings was instantly recognizable to me. Her hand rested on Fatima's shoulder and was greeted by Fatima's hand over it. "When I saw you at my door that day, I recognized your mother's hand in that collar. And then I looked at you, took a good look at your beautiful face, and I recognized Namunyak's features in you. Behind your pale skin, your bones and your blood are your mother's.

"When I first came to Tanganyika, I didn't know how to be African. My feet were soft, and I couldn't bear to go barefoot. Now I can't even feel my feet." Fatima stared at my boots. "And there you are, your feet always stuffed in men's boots. Your mother was the same way. I couldn't convince her of anything."

I was looking at my mother for the first time. In her I recognized my oval face and long neck, the way my lips puckered into a kiss, our broad foreheads, narrow noses, the almond-shaped eyes.

"I remember the first time your mother came to my shop, a satchel slung across her back. She did not say a word, simply walked up to my counter and opened the bag. It was filled with the most exquisite jewellery. Fine and delicate. I had never seen anything like it. I had never seen anyone like *her*. For three weeks, she stayed. I supplied the beads, and all day she'd work on her creations. She came back to me several more times. On her last visit, we went to a photographer before she left. I knew she would not return."

❋

Serafim switches off his recorder. "Fatima had this photograph all that time and chose to share it with you only then? Two years after you first met?"

"You do not see," I say, reluctant to show him how disappointed I am in what he is suggesting.

"What is it I'm missing?" Serafim asks.

"Only then did I understand what Fatima was giving me permission to do."

Serafim

I'VE ALWAYS FALLEN ASLEEP to sounds. Often to the sounds of
cars or people on the streets or shouting in their apartments.
Here, these sounds mix with the waves rolling farther and
farther across the sand. But it wasn't like that yesterday. My
head is heavy and fogged in the grey hotel room. I rub my eyes;
a shooting pain surges to my forehead. There are empty bottles
on my night table. Beside them lies a mountain of ash and
cigarette butts crowding an ashtray. A boy stands by the sliding
door to my balcony. He is looking out, his finger racing with
beads of rain down the glass.

"Who are you?" I say, my throat slashed with razors. I wince,
swallow. But I know who he is.

"Cigarettes?" the boy asks. Today he is wearing only shorts and sandals.

"Who let you in?"

Boys like this were part of my growing up as well. They littered the streets, and for the right price anything could be bought.

"Vodka?" the boy says, raising an invisible bottle to his mouth and guzzling.

"Get out!"

The boy comes and stands at the foot of my bed. He's not afraid of me. My head feels like a boulder. I couldn't chase him even if I wanted to.

I sit up in bed, swing my dumb legs over the side. "What time is it?"

"Past two o'clock," the boy says. "Wednesday."

He's mad. I reach for my wristwatch. The boy walks out the door. I'm wearing my boxers, drenched in sweat, and I've slept on a made bed.

I've been out two full days, almost three. When I last met with Pó I insisted it couldn't have been that easy for the villagers to have embraced Zeca the way she described. She reprimanded me for my insincerity, for pressing her on how little she knew about Ezequiel. I couldn't push her any further than she would allow. I needed to be patient.

I stagger to the door, my head not yet able to send clear messages to my legs. I wedge a chair under the doorknob, bump into a wall before making it to the bathroom. Lights on, I see my chin and cheeks. My skin looks sallow. I blame it on the lighting. A vague memory of sending the boy for hash. I needed something to smooth out the hard edges after seeing Rosalia a second time. She had followed me to the beach. Thin, barefoot in a cropped T-shirt and jeans, she was jittery, possibly high. Her eyes were red and swollen. I asked if she had seen Ophelia. She spoke softly, asked for a cigarette. I tapped one out of the packet. Rosalia didn't answer my question. I saw the tear in the shoulder of her shirt and didn't press her. She gave a shy smile and took the whole pack from my hand. That was Sunday. Three whole days lost. It's been so long since I went on a drinking binge, and this local stuff is potent.

All my notes, pages and pages of them, have been torn out and are scattered around the bed and on the floor. Some are crumpled; others have lost their ordered place. I read an excerpt, one of my first meetings with Pó. In it she described the various graves robbed for albino bones. Pó has memorized the crimes. The police won't keep records, so she does.

The room spins. I lay back down on my bed and light a cigarette. The first drag sears my throat. I look for a drop of liquor—just to douse the flame, I say to myself. Nothing in any of the three bottles scattered on my nightstand and on the floor.

I'm thinking of the triggers. It is always the same thing, a woman, or not having one, to be exact. I hadn't been with a woman in a long while. I thought of Rosalia, how easy it could have been to bring her back to my room, to wake up with her legs knotted with mine, feel her breath on my neck as I slept.

The rain has slowed and the streets are left with a sweet smell. It's short-lived. In the dying afternoon, hawkers call out bargains, all the while packing up their unsold goods. The flies have returned to swarm around carcasses of meat. The smells of animal flesh and warm and spoiled fruit make me queasy. But I have not eaten in days and there is nothing to throw up. I try to breathe, calm my thoughts, focus on students wandering home from school in clumps. Some of them crowd stairways up to apartment buildings, hang over balconies. Their voices meld into a buzz in my head.

I need an espresso, a double, some fresh bread to fill my stomach.

I haven't seen Pó in a few days. I've been careless. I can't jeopardize her trust. I need her story to finish.

Rosalia stands outside the VIP Inn Beira, a swanky hotel near the bakery. She is preening under the awning, her compact held up over her forehead. She catches me looking. I'm about to cross the street when a well-dressed man stops to speak to her. I'll go to the bakery, clear my head. If Rosalia's still there on my way back, I'll ask about Ophelia.

Down a narrow street, I pass between the iron-barred windows and step inside Padaria Indico. The generator's buzz competes with a football game on the TV. Men have gathered, drinking their espressos and small tumblers of booze. They tear at bolos and chew with mouths open, chase everything down with a shot of clear liquor—gin, vodka, Cashu. Just the sight of the sour stuff makes my stomach churn.

I'm saved by the smells. When I was ten, I came down from the favela to live with my grandmother's friend, a baker who, on those first cool nights after my grandmother's death, let me sleep by the layered ovens. She helped in my schooling and I became hers, until a man came to share her bed when I was thirteen.

Without looking at the board above the counter, I order half a dozen buns and a few things from the hot table. The girl stuffs a foil container with rice and what looks like goat stew, the food I had simply pointed at through the glass. I order a double espresso and drink it while the girl packs up all the food.

Rosalia no longer stands by the hotel entrance.

By the time I arrive at the Grande Hotel it is getting dark. I lean against the mosque's wall, next to the Coca-Cola machine. I need a smoke before going up to see Pó. I'm uncertain what I will tell her.

Two women drag a plastic bucket with laundry inside. One of them, a person with albinism, is missing an arm. She was a young mother and hid under her bed. The attackers offered her child a chocolate bar to disclose her whereabouts. The bucket bumps and scrapes over the broken concrete surrounding the pool. The mechanical whine of the Coca-Cola machine melds with the songs of prayer vibrating from within the mosque. The women dump their clothing into the deep end of the pool, where the day's rain must have diluted the putrid water. I take a long drag, watch the women drop to their knees to knead and slap and twist their haul. The maimed woman keeps up with her friend. She uses her feet to grip the washboard, her one arm rolling and flipping an article of clothing. She puts her whole body into the task and I am filled with shame. I look up at Pó's balcony.

I wish Rosalia had remained at the hotel. If she knew exactly where Ophelia went every night, who she was meeting, I could share it with Pó. If I told Pó I was paying Rosalia to keep an eye out for Ophelia, make sure she was safe, it might relieve some of Pó's concerns, distract her from my absence. I throw my cigarette down and snuff it with my shoe.

I find Pó sitting on her three-legged stool. She does not stir. I place the bag of bread and food on her bed and move to my chair. "I'm sorry," I say.

Pó raises her hand to stop me. "You owe me nothing," she says.

I'm not certain that's true. The truth is, time is running out for us both.

I undo the top two buttons of my shirt to settle in. The heat in Pó's room is insufferable. I thought the day's rain would have cooled things off. Still, Pó is bundled up—layered in saris and a light blanket over her shoulders.

I press Record. "I have a few questions about Gorongosa."

"I said it before. Ezequiel was lost." Her voice is barely audible.

"Lost how?"

"He did not know where he was going."

"And you brought him home. Up to the mountain without a worry—"

"The world is full of fear. It is a burden."

"He made a home there with you?"

"It was never a home. A stopping place."

"I can understand that," I say.

"Can you?" she mumbles before shifting around to face me. I'm caught off guard.

"I know very little about you," she says, her voice low and drawn out.

"There isn't much to know," I say, and as I say it I know I'm opening myself up to more questions.

Pó leans in, waiting for me to elaborate.

"I never knew my parents," I tell her. "I was raised by my grandmother. I was cared for and loved. It was all I needed." There is some truth to my words. "And now I choose to live alone."

Pó nods. "You have no family. No one is waiting for you back home."

"My life is underwhelming, I guess."

"So you give yourself over to a story. But it is always someone else's story, isn't it?"

"You could say that."

"I once saw a boat floating out to sea," she says, her voice laboured. "Its rope was cut. No fisherman sat inside. I watched it all day. It moved with the current. Until it drifted out to sea and disappeared."

"You really should eat something," I say. I rise to unknot the bag of food. Finally, I just tear the plastic handles apart and lay out the buns atop her bed. When I lift the lid of rice and goat stew, a rich smell is released. I'm queasy and hot.

"I cannot eat. Leave it for Amalia," she says, struggling to get up.

I take a few steps toward her, ready to catch her if she should fall. Her whole body shakes.

"Forgive me if I am too tired to talk tonight."

I reach out to her and she takes hold of my forearm, presses down with her weight. She shuffles a few steps back into the room to sit on her bed.

"I do not have much time," she says.

"I'm here," I say.

Pó considers my words. She places her hands flat on her bedspread and smooths it out. She sits in silence. I'm afraid to move.

"Can I get you something? Some water?"

She shakes her head. "Will you stay a little longer?"

It is my turn to nod. "Can I ask you something? When I first met you, you said white men have always told your story."

Pó closes her eyes.

"Why me, then?"

She takes a deep breath. "When I told you Emmanuel's story. How he had his left arm, his right hand, and part of his jaw hacked off. How he killed himself after that, too afraid to speak. I heard you snap your pencil. You care." She smiles.

Ezequiel

I'M CROUCHING IN THE CORNER of my room. I don't know how long I've been here. My eyes have been open for a time, but I can't seem to take anything in. This is my room. That is my bed. Through the window, I see a plastic bag tossing in the wind.

In bare feet, I climb the stairs out to the backyard, open the gate to collect the bag. Before I can catch it in mid-air, it floats down the narrow walkway and skips out onto the road. I'm distracted by geese swooping in formation up above. They disappear, cut off by the angle of the neighbour's roof. I make my way onto the sidewalk. *There they are.* From my backyard, I used to watch birds migrating. Pigeons flew by too, and wrens and sparrows, though it was impossible to identify what kinds of birds they were when they appeared as colourless specks fizzing across the sky.

Why did I come outside?

A woman is trailing a bundle-buggy behind her. She raises her hand as if she recognizes me. I cross the road. I continue walking toward Dundas Street. "I need milk," I say out loud. Senhor Leonildo's convenience store on the corner opens early, but when I tug at the door it is locked. Peering inside, I don't recognize anything. I see half a dozen large chairs with foot sinks. The sign reads NAIL SPA. I don't know where Senhor Leonildo's store has gone. I'm certain it was here yesterday. I cross the street. Maybe if I stand on the grass of Trinity Bellwoods Park, I will get a better sense of where I am. A car screeches to a halt. The driver yells profanities and veers around me.

If I just sit for a minute or two, I'll be able to get my bearings and figure out how to get home. People are bundled up, making their way to work. They see me and look away, stepping off the sidewalk onto the road before moving east, I think it is, on Dundas Street toward the downtown. I find a concrete bench and stretch out on my side, my head against the seat, my cheek on its surface. I cannot stop my teeth from rattling.

Which way is home?

"Senhor Zeca?" a man says.

There is nowhere to hide. The man's face is familiar. He says words but they are not formed in sentences: *John. Live upstairs. You okay? Cold out here.* He places his winter coat over my shoulders. When he speaks, his breath turns to mist. "It's November, too cold to be out without a coat."

I see I am wearing only boxer shorts and an undershirt.

"I'll take you home," he says.

Safely in my bedroom, I bite my lip till I taste blood. I need to go to the bathroom. I can't hold it, but I can't get up. My hands are at my mouth, cupped to the shape of the instrument I used to hold. I hear the notes in my head, "O Silver Moon," to conjure a much happier time and place. *I saw Pó in the water and I followed.*

I hear the thud of the basement door closing. The nurse covers her nose with her forearm. I'm not certain how she manages to get me into the tub, how she straps me down to a plastic chair from some medical supply house. The shower head hovers over me. I close my eyes and breathe through my mouth. I gag and my stomach tightens. I pretend I do not feel ashamed. I want to scream. I can't, the cry stuck like a hot coal burning in my throat.

"And when I'm done I'll get you a fresh change of clothes. You'll feel much better."

It's useless to ask her to leave.

"You were due for a bath, anyways," she says.

I look down. The nurse has covered my genitals with a face-cloth. The smell of coconut shampoo drowns out the other smells that have washed down the drain.

She works up lather around my neck and under my arms, and the smell of geranium and lavender oils tickles my nose. Mother Anke has told me I'm getting too tall to bathe in a barrel; I am a young man now and everything needs to be in perfect order, for this is what God demands of us—perfection in prayer and devotion. The sun goes down, a shocking pink streaming through the treetops. A dot appears in the distance, at the top of the hill where the road narrows. I am certain it is Papa Gilberto returning from his trip to Porto Amélia. I recognize his horse's gallop kicking up dirt behind it. Papa dismounts in the clearing. He does not see me. I submerge into the barrel so that only the top of my head and my eyes are above water. His clothing is covered in red dirt from the long journey. He removes his hat and his hair is sweaty, plastered against his forehead. He walks toward the barrel and I notice the worry in his eyes. I sink under the surface.

The moment Papa Gilberto dips his hands into the water, I pop up. Papa Gilberto pretends he is surprised, and I love him more than I ever have. He kisses my forehead. "My little fish is getting big."

"I'm washing up for my birthday," I say.

"Is that today?" he asks, smiling, before splashing his face and neck with water. Papa Gilberto notices my slingshot on the bench by my towel. "Such beautiful work."

"A gift from Lázaro."

Papa takes the soap from my hand and begins to build lather

between his palms. I think it is to wash his face, but instead, he lays his sudsy hands on my head and begins to dig his fingers into my hair. I close my eyes. When I open them, I see Papa's have welled up. I plunge under the surface.

※

Most evenings we share the fire and food between us, away from the other villagers. I have been here six weeks and look forward to this time of the day most. I help carry Fatima to her sleeping mat. To thank me, Pó returns to the fire and prepares coffee. It is weak and full of grounds, but I don't tell her. Pó holds the small elephant carving in her hand. Her fingers move around it.

"I am happy to have found this place."

"We are all safe here," she says.

It would be safer to move off the mountain, I think. Perhaps cross the border into Rhodesia—but I know Pó will never leave Fatima behind, and Fatima is too weak to travel.

"They all left," I say, poking at the fire. I tell her that when I was thirteen the workers fled the mission; all that remained were a couple of goats wandering in the clearing, gourds and spilled baskets, ropes scattered outside the workers' huts. "The war was closing in. I tried to fill the emptiness in the pit of my stomach. Everything will go back to the way it always was, I kept saying. The workers would return to the mission, Papa would spread the word of God, and Mother Anke would get better."

"Your mother was not well?"

It is difficult to answer Pó's question. "She was *out of her head*, Papa said."

I picture Mother Anke lowering herself into the chair by the well, lost in her thoughts. She had demanded the well be built and Papa Gilberto had humoured her. He knew there would be no water. But when the walls collapsed on a worker, Papa put a stop to construction. To appease her, he built a circular stone fence and even fashioned a bucket on a pulley. Some mornings she would lower the bucket into the well, draw it back up, empty.

I picture Mother Anke sitting in the chair, her eyes glued to the dirt road, her foot tapping the ground, as if waiting for something to happen or someone to appear.

Come here, Mother Anke said, *let me take a closer look at you.* She brushed my cheek with the back of her hand. The news that morning of an increased military presence to crush FRELIMO guerrillas had given her a glimmer of hope. She appeared much larger spread out in her chair. *I have some mussiro paste for my little man.*

It burns, I told her. *I don't want it.* She had laced the paste with bleach.

It beautifies the skin.

I tried to pull away. She held firm.

Ezequiel, stop! We'll be leaving this place soon. You need to be ready.

"Fatima calls you a scribbler. I can hear you at night. I like the sound you make."

Pó gathers her shuka and blanket and steps to the fire to pour me more coffee. "What do you write about?"

"The people left behind."

The war spreads like a bush fire. Pó has no idea that it will catch up to us. It always does.

"I have been here long enough," I say. "I must leave soon. Will you come with me?" I fear her answer.

"Fatima wants to die here. She believes this is God's garden."

"Do you believe that?"

"Anything is possible."

I do not sleep well after Pó leaves me by the fire. The world is a big place, but Commander Fonseca will eventually find me; he is never far behind. All night, sudden jolts from the first sign of sleep have me reaching for my rifle. Land mines explode in my head, bloated bodies drift downriver, the image of Beatriz with the barrel of a gun in her mouth haunts me. The smells and the sounds cling to my skin.

Going down the mountain's side has become easier. I've built up my strength in the time I have been here.

I follow Pó down the narrow path. I am far slower, but my eagerness today steadies my pace. I have another twenty feet to climb down when I see her at the pool's bank. She slips out of her shuka and I see the flash of her white figure. I swallow. Clumsily, I scurry down the last few feet, trip over some vines. I look out and see that she is smiling to herself.

I cross over the rocks and lower myself on one knee. I take her shuka into my hand, close my fist around it. I bring it up to my nose, take in her sweet smell.

I unbutton my shirt, unbuckle my belt, my pants drop to my ankles.

Pó breaks the surface and freezes.

I can't swim, but far greater than my fear is the desire to touch her skin. I step into the water.

Pó

"Amalia, stop playing with that record player. I need your young eyes to thread a needle."

"I'm fixing the music box," Amalia says. She throws herself onto the mattress. The glass beads I had separated by colour are sent into the air.

"Filha!"

"I'll help," she says, and begins sorting the beads into small piles. "We're almost running out."

"You will have to go to the market soon and get some more."

I only ever work with glass beads, as my mother and Simu had before me. I bring my hand up to touch the beaded collar my mother once wore.

"I don't like going to the market. They say mean things."

"Who does?"

"Mwanito makes fun of me. He calls this the ghost hotel and I'm its ghost keeper."

"You can't listen to nonsense." I remember Mwanito as a boy. He once lived in the Grande Hotel, in Block C. Overnight the hotel became a safe place for refugees from what was once Rhodesia during their civil war. The common rule for living in the Grande Hotel is respect. As squatters, the refugees are given the nickname *whato muno*—not from here. Like the albinos, they are not accepted in Beira. Mwanito shed his skin and has reinvented himself. "Mwanito is not a bad man, filha. He's a young man. He does not understand the world." It strikes me then that I did not wake up to the scratching song of women sweeping the courtyard. The hotel grounds are deserted. I see a few children pulling a calf up the beach road and a load of soldiers together in the bed of a truck. The truck swerves, and with each jolt the men in the back roar in laughter, only to resume their shouting and singing with their rifles raised high.

"How come you don't sit with the other women to make jewellery anymore?" Amalia says. "They miss you."

The doctor who visits twice a year has told me that the lesions on my neck and shoulders are cancerous and the disease is now in my blood. I cannot tell Amalia that it is safer for me to stay inside my room now. Murderers lurk in Beira's crowds. They have heard that my bones will fetch a high price on the market. They will see I am not as strong as I once was and they will pounce.

"The necklace I am wearing will be yours one day. My mother never put similar colours next to each other. That was her way. A dark bead is always set against a lighter colour. And every bead has meaning."

Amalia holds up a large, flat beaded disc. "What is this one for?"

"It's for young girls like you," I say, poking her belly. She smiles.

"And this one?" Amalia thrusts a red bead up close to my face so I can see.

"That colour is for bravery and blood. Blue is the colour of the sky. It provides water for the cattle. Green for the grass. Black is the colour of the people."

❋

As I wait for Serafim's visit, I think about what I have left to share with him, which parts will remain mine.

❋

I stood at the pool's bank and slipped out of my shuka. The mountain air was cool. Two steps in and the water met my knees. Two more steps and the water lapped my thighs. I spread my arms and thrust myself into the water. A chill. A rush.

When I surfaced, Ezequiel had crossed over the wet rocks and was kneeling by my shuka.

I took another plunge, stayed under as long as I could. I surfaced breathlessly to the rumble of the waterfall.

Ezequiel now stood at the edge of the water. I turned and swam away from him, towards the waterfall.

"What do you want?" I said, my voice as calm as I could make it.

He did not answer but dropped my shuka to the ground.

"I can't swim," he said.

"Trust the water," I said.

He took one step onto a slippery stone. I could see him, arms wide out, trying to balance. I swam closer to him.

He was unbuttoning his shirt. His belt was next, the slap of leather loud. His pants dropped to his ankles. He stepped out of his pants and onto another rock.

He took one step into the water. Then another. I swam out farther. When I surfaced, the water reached his waist. I held his hand and led him into the pool. Three, four, five steps more. He tugged back and wouldn't go any deeper. "Trust me," I said.

"One step after another," I heard him whisper.

The sun was disappearing. I lay next to Ezequiel on a bed of moss. Giant ferns surrounded us, their tips dipping into the water.

"You are quiet," I said.

"I don't want anything to change."

We had been there all day. I had told him about my child-hood, about Simu and Koinet and Lebo.

Ezequiel lay motionless. Quiet.

"I don't remember things as clearly," he finally said, swallow-ing hard. "The workers on the mission had left. Papa grew a beard, I remember that. He wore a brave face when he fried eggs every night for dinner. That was all he knew how to cook, which was fine with me because he fried them until their edges turned bronze. Mother Anke sat across from Papa. She did not eat. She looked smaller, diminished in a way I couldn't understand."

Ezequiel talked about Macaco and his men and when he was captured by the Portuguese. He would begin to tell me what he had seen and then his lips would close. Side by side, our arms and legs touching, I watched his chest rise and fall. It slowed sometimes and I thought his burden had been lightened.

Ezequiel moved away from me. He sat up, curled into himself.

"What is it?"

Metal flashed through the open spaces in the canopy of trees.

He covered his ears and rocked gently. "My rifle. Give me my rifle!" His eyes were on fire.

I did not understand. I was afraid. I crouched beside him, held him tight, until the rocking slowed.

"He is near," Ezequiel said.

"Shhh," I said.

"The Commander is near," he sobbed, his head dropped into his hands. "It's over."

It had been a while since a plane had come so close, but it had been no different than the other times.

"He'll find us," he mumbled.

I felt his panic and held him tight. My shuka turned into a pillow to prop up his head. I left his side and brought back water.

His eyelids closed, softly. I kissed his forehead. "I taste sadness," I said.

Kwazi was sent down the side of the mountain for supplies. He returned with rumours. Both FRELIMO soldiers and the Portuguese army were looking for clear vantage points in the area. He did not know what these groups represented. I bribed him with honey to keep the news to himself.

Serafim

I STAND BY THE SHORE watching the waves roll in, churning sand, debris half-hidden in the ocean's foam. Using my toes, I wedge one shoe off, then the other. I roll up each sock and tuck one in each shoe, far enough from where the water reaches dry sand. Rolling up the cuffs of my pants, I take those first few steps into the cold water. There is immediate relief.

This may be my last meeting with Pó. I will be leaving Beira soon. Taking with me all the effort that Pó has put into crafting her life.

A wave crashes against my shins. I stagger back. My calves are pulled by the undertow into deeper water, knee-high.

Sunday, and most of the city is closed now. There are hardly any lights except the blue glow from fluorescent bulbs in billiards halls or all-night cafés. Gradually I become aware of only the Grande Hotel. When I stand on my balcony it appears as a black hole erased from the city. I think of the dream realized when it was built. No money was spared. The idea was that they would come to safari in luxury, feel compelled to stay in this unknown city, and the place would fill them with wonder.

Ezequiel

I CAN'T SLEEP. It is cold and gloomy. I pace around. From kitchen to bedroom to living room, back to kitchen. A full circle before I begin again. Bedroom to living room to kitchen.

In my dream, I confessed to Pó. I disposed of the girls in different ways. I let one girl slip into a river, the current dragging her somewhere she could not be recognized. I pulled another victim into the woods to be covered in a shallow grave of loam. Abel watched me hoist the first girl, the one who worked the tobacco fields, the one I wrapped in the Commander's bloodied sheets, into the back of the jeep. I was being tested. He did not offer help. I drove to the swamp, not far off from the base. I carried her like a groom carries his bride. I sank into the loam and mud and papyrus. She became weightless in the water. I could not go deeper, afraid there would be a drop and I would drown. Her body was set adrift. The sheets unravelled. My feet sank in deeper so that the water was at my chest. I panicked and went under. Regaining firmer footing—a stone or log—I gasped for air. I opened my eyes and saw the bloated head of a corpse float by, its features unrecognizable.

Bedroom to living room. Kitchen . . .

❋

I arrived at the foot of Gorongosa in early November. It is now March—a full year since I ran from Dar es Salaam to find this place. With every day the anxiety that comes with remaining on the mountain builds. They will find me.

"Fatima is not well," I whisper.

"Machinga has prepared medicine."

"The medicine won't help her."

Later, as we sit with Fatima, she tells us it is time to leave.

"Where?" I ask.

"Beira. It has been arranged. You will be married in God's house."

"No, Fatima. I will stay with you. Ezequiel is here to help."

"I want you both to go. You have cared for me. It is more than any daughter would do. But you must begin your life. I have lived mine."

I dream of setting up a new mission across the border, where things might be safer. There will be goats and chickens and crops. People will come and gather. Many are looking for a better life. "We will go," I say.

"Love her as God intends," Fatima says.

I look outside. In the morning, the air of the mountain is cool and moist and the sun is just tipping the rain-forested slopes. We leave in silence and reach the ranch in time to find John Wright loading the cattle onto the bed of his truck.

A week before, Fatima sent Kwazi to arrange things with the cattle rancher. He has agreed to drive us to Beira. He has been paid. He tilts his hat and opens the door to the cab of his truck.

The journey will take twelve hours, he tells us. "That is, if all goes well."

"Are you selling your cattle?" I ask.

"I'm selling everything I own," he replies. His tone suggests that any further questions or attempt at conversation will not be welcome. He will talk when he chooses.

We're an hour in when he tells us he raises Brangus cattle, a breed well-suited to the climate of the mountain. For years he's taken the cattle to market across the swollen Pungwe River by pontoon, where a dozen or so men, wise in the currents of the river, use bamboo poles to push the pont upstream before catching the current and guiding the craft to the opposite bank.

From there it will be over a couple of hundred kilometres of bumpy road to Beira.

Pó is quiet. She saw Beira once. Padre Theuns, the parish priest, drove them to Gorongosa when they'd left Dar es Salaam. It is the only thing she says to me during the long journey. I do not share my fears of what it means to enter Beira, a foothold of the Portuguese army. I try to block the idea from my mind.

There are washed-out roads, crumbling bridges, but we have yet to come across a military checkpoint. Close to midnight, we enter the city and pull up to the church's gates. The cattle are restless, held tightly for so long on the back of the truck.

"This is where you get off. We leave in two days. Noon," Wright says, and drives off.

Pó is walking across the church grounds. She collapses near the rectory door, cocoons herself in her shuka and a blood-red capulana—a wedding gift from Fatima. "The church is closed. Can you try to find him?"

"Wait here. I won't go far." The first man I stumble upon is derelict, curled up on a sheet of cardboard. "Can you tell me where I can find Padre Theuns?"

The man blinks, raises his open palm, and offers me a wry smile.

A little farther down the road that leads to the beach, another man smoking a cigarette points to the bar. Pó once described him as a white man who didn't look like a priest. I wasn't sure what that meant. He was a man in his early forties with a

scruffy appearance, unkempt beard, and Pó said if I could hear
him speak I'd hear a South African accent.

Padre Theuns is alone, slumped in a chair. He is wearing
a faded Jimi Hendrix T-shirt, the neck stretched so wide that
part of his shoulder is bare. The tattered sandal on his left
foot is held together with twine.

"Padre Theuns. Fatima sent us."

At first, the priest does not seem to register who I'm referring to.

"She sent me here with Pó. She said you would marry us."

"Ah, the Goan queen has sent you with her beautiful albino.
How is she?" he slurs. He mumbles to himself, mixing what I
assume is Afrikaans with Portuguese.

"Forgive me, Padre Theuns, but you don't look like a priest."

"Didn't Jesus wear sandals? Buy me a drink and I'll show
you what kind of priest I am."

It is dark, perhaps two o'clock in the morning, as I help Father
Theuns home. The streets are empty, save the few street people
who live in cardboard boxes.

"Let me confess something to you."

"Isn't it meant to work the other way round?"

We stop in the middle of a road. He claps his hands to the
sides of my face and holds me still. "These government officials
and military men, they are evil. The derelicts, the impoverished,
the thieves and prostitutes, these are true and honest people."

"I understand."

"Listen to me," he says, his sour breath making me sick. "I serve them, not this ugly war or this country that is being swarmed by tsetse-fly politicians. They have turned purple and engorged from sucking our blood."

"We are almost home," I say, directing him forward. The church is a block away.

"We have no home," he says.

Padre Theuns embraces Pó. He fumbles with his keys in the keyhole and hands them to me.

"You will sleep in my bed tonight," he says. "What use is a bed if you can't share it with someone." He winks at me as I lower him to the living room couch. He insists he is more comfortable right here on the couch.

"You need rest after such a long journey. And you need to be ready at dawn, when I will marry you in this church of God, as Fatima wishes."

I look into the bedroom. Pó is fast asleep. The bottoms of her feet are dirty, dark against her skin and the clean sheets.

Padre Theuns is dressed in his vestments when he enters his room. He sprinkles us and the bed with holy water. It is enough to wake us.

The ceremony is simple. It lasts no more than five minutes. There are only two candles on the altar, a few words, and a bond sealed with a kiss. Pó is wearing the same shuka she has worn this whole journey. She covers her head with a crimson capulana as her veil. It was what Fatima had taught her to do in church. No rings are exchanged, and Padre Theuns assures us it is only a ceremonial formality, unnecessary; we can buy two gold rings whenever we can afford it.

"When will you leave?" Padre Theuns asks.

"Tomorrow at noon," I say. "A driver will pick us up at the church."

Pó blows out the candles at the ends of the altar.

"Well then, I must give you both a proper wedding gift."

"No, Padre Theuns," Pó says. "Senhora Fatima asked me to give you this."

Padre Theuns wedges the envelope open and slips one of the bills into his pocket. The others he gives back to Pó. "That is all I need to say a mass for Fatima and for the two of you. The rest you keep."

She tries to shove the envelope back in the priest's hands, but Padre Theuns will have none of it.

"When Fatima and you first came to my church almost two years ago, she gave this church more money than anyone has ever given. It went to fatten the Archbishop and his political friends."

"Thank you, Father. You are a good man," I say.

"You must leave before the church ladies come to cook me breakfast and make my bed. They are spies for the Archbishop.

Before you go, Pó, rummage through the pile of clothing in the rectory office. They are meant to go to the poor, but you will be safer in the streets of Beira with clothing more suited to the city."

"How can we ever repay you?" Pó says.

"By being true to each other."

Padre Theuns gives Fulvio, a young Italian, the task of delivering us to the shuttered Grande Hotel. Senhor João, the overseer, has kept things guarded and in their place in case the war ends and people return to visit Mozambique on safari.

Through the car window Pó looks out onto the streets of Beira. She wears a white skirt that slips up to mid-thigh, a floral shirt, large-framed sunglasses, and a floppy hat. The only thing she doesn't like are the sandals, which feel flimsy, she says, not heavy and grounded like the combat boots she is used to wearing.

I know Pó's thoughts are someplace else, up on Mount Gorongosa with Fatima. Even though the old woman asked us not to return, Pó and I, without ever discussing it, know we will climb the mountain once again.

"One more day and we'll be home," I say. "Stop!" I cry, tapping the headrest behind Fulvio. He slows at a storefront. The large sign above the caged window reads RELOJOARIA ZURIQUE.

"Why are we stopping?" Pó says.

"I'm going to buy you a wedding ring."

Fulvio is reluctant to allow us out of the car. He has strict instructions to deliver us safely to Senhor João, but I open the door as the car is moving and Fulvio is forced to stop.

Pó's eyes are glued to another shop across the road, the lettering on the sign large enough that she can read it: OPTICA ZURIQUE.

"Come," I say, and lead her across the road.

A diminutive man greets us when we walk in. He stands behind the counter but does not look up. He wears tiny spectacles, their wire arms curling behind his large ears. "Can I help you?" he asks.

"I'd like to buy spectacles for my wife."

Pó looks bewildered.

The small man who smells of cough syrup comes around the counter to stand in front of her. "I am Osvaldo. Your hat, Madame."

He conceals his shock very well—her afro-textured hair, shorn close to her head, palest of orange. He is trying to pin down her eyes, which dart side to side.

"Nystagmus. It's quite common in people like you." He says it without the slightest judgment. He moves to the shop window and draws the curtains. He locks the shop's door. "I might be able to do something," he says.

I draw the curtains to the side and give Fulvio a sign that we are well. Fulvio slaps the steering wheel and taps his wristwatch.

"Sit here, Madame," the man says. Pó sits in the chair, her hands clenching the sides of her skirt. The man swings a machine that looks like a large mask into place in front of her. "Eyeglasses won't give you twenty-twenty vision, but in some cases they can help."

As Senhor Osvaldo snaps lenses of varying magnifications in front of Pó's eyes, asking her to read the chart over his shoulder, I spot an old record player in the corner. It stands on a table, where underneath, a brass rack holds thirty or so albums. I let my fingers rest on the turntable, sweep them across the arm to caress the crank.

"Do you mind?" I ask, squatting to flip through his collection of albums.

I turn the crank. I place the album on the turntable and locate the exact groove that indicates the song I want to hear. I lower the needle and the speakers crackle. Then it begins . . . I don't see the optometrist fitting Pó with a pair of spectacles, their brass frames thin wires. All I hear is music. All I see is Papa Gilberto closing the shutters to his office and locking them. As he reaches over his desk to shoo the moths away and dim the oil lamp, I catch his lips curling into a smile and know he is watching over me. He picks up the oil lamp in one hand and reaches out to me with his free hand. Papa helps me up and I hug his waist; the weight of his arm drops over my shoulder. He smiles down at me and I bury my face in his side. I smell his night smell—the faint trace of soap on his shirt—and feel the hair of his arm brushing against my ear and cheek. I am too big but I step onto his shoes so I can ride his feet out of the room.

"This may seem an odd request, but would you consider selling me this record player?" The minute I ask I feel stupid for doing so. It must mean something to him.

"Your price?" he says.

Crossing the road to Fulvio's car, I have the record player tucked under my arm. A convoy of military trucks is passing. Pó presses herself against me. The green caterpillar of army trucks and tanks has been given a clear path on the road, cars pulling to the side to let them pass.

I can't move. I hear Pó tell me to breathe deeply. *Can you see Mount Gorongosa, Ezequiel? It's close,* she says. I hoist the record player securely against my hip.

"There's no escaping them," I whisper.

"Zeca, listen. We're going to walk to the car and we are going to be safe," she says.

Cars are honking, swerving to be clear of us in the middle of the road. A man sticks his head out his window and yells something. I can feel hands on me. Pó is shoving me, trying to get me to move. People have stopped to witness the commotion.

At the end of the convoy a luxury car passes, its driver's window half-opened. It jolts and stops beside me. I look straight at Abel as he lowers his sunglasses.

Pó

"He placed the eyeglasses on my nose," I tell Serafim. "For the first time in my life I was able to see clearly—colours and shapes."

"I can't imagine what that must have been like," Serafim says.

"I fought hard not to cry. I didn't want tears to blur my sight. I could see Ezequiel sitting next to a record player. His head was pressed back against the counter. He wept, I think now, for the memory of a man who was his father. And at that moment all I thought was, *This is the way the world looks; this is the way the world was meant to be.*"

❋

Fulvio sat in his car and honked until I thought I would go deaf. Ezequiel's feet appeared stuck to the tar in the middle of the road. The military trucks sped by us and Ezequiel shook. I had to use my head like a goat to push him into Fulvio's car.

Senhor João was waiting for us. He helped me drag Ezequiel into the hotel while Fulvio hid his car. The man did not ask questions. Everything had been arranged with Padre Theuns. He had been paid and he understood discretion. "I was here when the Grande opened in 1954, and I was here in 1963 when it closed," Senhor João said, like a guide. He pretended he did not see the shell-shocked look on Ezequiel's face. He told us that he had become the hotel's unofficial watchman, never asking the owners to pay him, even though on the few visits they made to the hotel they recognized his role in keeping the hotel safe from intruders.

Senhor João possessed keys to every room. He understood how to control the water supply and electricity panels. Because of this power, he had influence with people in Beira.

The hotel had the soft angles and clean lines that had taken the place of older colonial buildings in the new city of Beira. The furniture was shrouded with white sheets. Senhor João pressed the button for something he called an elevator, but I had already moved towards the wide circular staircase that floated upward, towards the ceiling of glass. Fulvio carried the record player and a bag with a couple of record albums. Ezequiel leaned up against the staircase. He looked pale and his clothing stuck to his sweating body. I kept looking up to the glass dome. With my eyeglasses on, I saw the metal and the light in a very new way. Senhor João took the lead and directed us past the landings of pink-and-white floors. "Turn right. I told Padre Theuns I'd give you the very best room. Here it is," he said.

The room was furnished with a wrought iron canopy bed, wooden side tables and chairs, a dresser of drawers. Senhor João swung the shutters to the side. He opened glass doors. Still in a daze, Ezequiel sat down on the bed. I walked onto the balcony that spread wide above an empty swimming pool and the hotel grounds.

"Is he well?" Senhor João asked.

"He is tired from the journey," I replied.

"I will leave you alone, then. All electricity and running water has been turned off. Do not stand on the balcony. Remember to draw the shutters when you light the candle. It's best no one knows you are here."

Ezequiel was already asleep. I lay beside him.

I woke to the sound of music. I looked up at my husband, standing by his record player, weeping.

I folded back the shutters and the morning sun spilled into the room. I shielded my eyes with my hand. When my eyes adjusted, I leaned over the balcony and reached out to the sea.

"Get away from there!" Ezequiel came from behind and dragged me back into the room. He nestled his chin on my shoulder and breathed heavily.

"Everything's fine," I said.

I had seen the gardens, the dry ground, the tiled swimming pool a silent blue. Fruit bats twanged over the mango trees. The perfume of their blossoms mixed with the ripe smell of fallen fruit fermenting on the ground. I had looked out to where the Buzi and the Pungwe Rivers met, then out over the expanse of the Indian Ocean. Its deepest parts turned indigo. Ezequiel kissed my neck, the back of my head. He pressed his body into mine and held tight as if he would never let go.

✸

Amalia sleeps with me in my bed. I do not want to wake her. I listen to her shallow breaths. Often, when I cannot find sleep, I look at her beside me and let the sounds coming from her slumber, the hisses and soft gurgles, lull me, until I can almost cry. The elephant carving remains caged in her delicate fingers.

Simu taught me it was best to always speak the truth. Amalia knows her real mother was an albino, no more than fifteen when she got pregnant. She was unwed and already shunned in her village. She found her way to the Grande Hotel and stayed with me. I told Amalia that we were born in the same way—to mothers who loved us but could not take care of us.

"Has the sun gone away, Alma?" Amalia asks, batting her eyelashes and stretching her arms above her head. Her fingertips touch the wrought iron headboard. She has grown to look like her mother. Her cheeks are fatter now—the same grin, the same eyes.

"Almost, filha," I whisper, stroking the soft skin under her chin.

"Has the scribbler left?" she asks.

"His name is Serafim, and he will return again tonight."

Amalia does not like that I share my stories with others. Four or five scribblers, all men, have come and gone over the years. Serafim is the first one to insist I tell my story from the beginning. It is the only way to capture its meaning, he says. I've already revealed more to him than I ever have before. I pull Amalia close to me. She reaches behind and places her hand on my neck. She touches my sores carefully. I do not flinch. I do not want to frighten her.

Later that evening, from my perch on the balcony, I see Serafim outside the hotel grounds, caught in a crowd of people, among bundles of cloth, chickens and goats, bottles of water, smouldering fires and rusted cars that barely roll down the unpaved roads. Children surround him offering their services as porters or begging for money. He breaks through and walks along the edge of the garbage-filled pool. How clear the pool must have been once, when the hotel had just opened and it seemed like all its promise was held in that large rectangle of unnatural blue. Now in the glow of the Coca-Cola machine, the murky water that has collected in the deep end is the colour of blood.

I turn from the ocean. Amalia is tinkering with the record player. It is encased in black leather. The brass handle clips onto the lid, where she enjoys tracing the gold-embossed letters, DECCA, with her fingers. Convinced she will get the disc to spin, her slender fingers pinch the arm, while her other hand grips the crank and turns. She is a determined child, and part of me is certain she will succeed one day. Nothing would give me more joy than to hear music lifting into the air. I can see Ezequiel cranking the machine, *right there, in that very spot*, I think, as he lowers the arm over the record that circles and crackles until the sound shoots out. A woman's voice took him away to a place that was safe and familiar. I could only watch and love him because it was all I had; he was never mine.

"I am leaving in a few days."

It is that time.

He slips his tape recorder from his pocket and presses Record.

Sitting on the edge of my bed, I thumb the frayed edge of my shuka. I reach over to light the lantern atop the stacked crates by my bedside. This is my room and everything in it is all I have: a bed, a makeshift nightstand, the chair Serafim sits in, two cardboard boxes that hold my things, and a broken record player on the floor in the corner.

"Where is Amalia?" Serafim asks.

Ophelia was not around this morning to watch the children. Amalia went to visit all the hotel blocks, hoping to find someone who had seen her.

"She'll be back soon," I say, but there is a burning sensation rising in my throat and gut. I want Amalia near me, close by. I wind the loose threads from my shuka around my finger and tug. The hem comes undone, the edge raw.

"Whenever you're ready," Serafim says.

"When I had healed, the boy, Kwazi, helped me bring the record player down from the mountain," I say, wiping my lenses with my sleeve. "I knew how important music was to Ezequiel, and I hoped he'd come back to claim it."

"I'm not sure I understand."

"Ezequiel and I went back up the mountain together, but I came down alone."

Serafim walks over to stand beside me on the balcony. He places his hand on my shoulder. Only now, before he leaves, does he touch me. It feels good to have the weight of his hand on me.

Ezequiel

Pó sat by Fatima's side watching the rise and fall of the woman's chest.

It was a vigil. Machinga entered the hut to relieve Pó. She remained with Vasco, when everyone else in the village had moved down the mountain or closer to the Rhodesian border. Machinga and Vasco were too old to leave. Kwazi remained to look after his grandparents. He ran off the mountain to visit his parents and returned with necessary provisions.

I didn't recall much about our return home from Beira, two weeks before. Pó said we were stopped at three different checkpoints by the Portuguese army. They were looking for FRELIMO insurgents. Pó held me tight, kept me quiet. A scan of the flashlight beam, a quick check of the vehicle's interior and underneath it, and we moved on. I remained in a state of terror the whole time, looking over my shoulder, searching for Abel.

Fatima died in the evening. A couple of days before, I had found a soft patch of soil on one of the top slopes. With Kwazi's help, I dug a hole deep enough to bury her. The busy work took the worry away from my troubled mind. I knew things could not remain the same. The war would catch up to me, to Pó. The visit to Beira made that clear. We needed a way out.

Vasco sits at his grinder, pressing the blade and sweeping it from side to side with balance and precision.

"Do you have a proverb for me today, old man?" I ask. It's a game we play. Vasco translates a Bantu proverb into Portuguese and I have up to ten questions to help me decipher the proverb's meaning. I sit on a bench directly across from Vasco and think of Papa Gilberto.

"A stick one bends while it is still green," he says. I was hoping for one of the funny ones, like my favourite: Stroke your dog and he will steal eggs.

"I'm afraid I need something to lift my spirits."

"You asked. You must live your life, Zeca. But to do so you must defeat your demons."

He pats the bench next to him. I shift closer, my arm brushing his side. He rests his hand on my thigh.

"Now. A stick one bends while it is still green."

"I don't know where to begin."

"Pó. Stay close to her," he says quickly, wiping his sleeve across his mouth to sop up the dribble. "I have Machinga. Fatima had her God. You have Pó. She is all you need."

Sparks jump from the steel blade only to disappear at Vasco's bare feet. His hands remain steady with the effort of his work.

Pó is sitting across from the fire. Her whole body is covered in white, shrouded in pure mourning.

"We must bury Fatima. I have her grave ready."

"No," Pó says. "I will do what my aunt Simu did for my mother. Simu slaughtered a goat and covered my mother in its fat and blood. Five moons later, my mother was gone. This is our way."

Kwazi returns carrying a duiker around his neck. It is one of the antelopes that live at the top of Mount Gorongosa, and because this is a sacred killing, the boy did not have to travel down the mountain to kill it. He drops the animal on the ground.

Pó and Machinga begin to carve.

"Fatima will go to church one final time," Pó says.

It is late. With bloodied hands, Machinga slips into the hut and helps Pó drag Fatima's naked body outside. Disease had eaten away at her and she had turned thin. Her body has stiffened, but they manage to prop Fatima up in her wheel-chair. Machinga threads a sari under Fatima's arms and across her chest before securing the woman's torso to the back of the chair. Pó places Fatima's lace veil over her head, and with her body slightly askew, Fatima is ready.

Pó pushes the chair and makes her way along the narrow path to the clearing and the smouldering fire that is tended by Vasco and Kwazi. As we approach, Vasco stands away from the fire, leaving Kwazi to poke his stick at the wood, lifting red embers into the black sky.

Pó circles the fire with Fatima in her chair, the same way she has done every Sunday since they arrived, but this time Pó sings a song. I know it. It is the lullaby Simu had sung to Pó as a child, the same song Pó sang to the elephant calf.

✸

I'm singing a song that is on the radio as I set the table. My voice cracks. John, the renter upstairs who helped me home the other day, has been leaving meals outside my basement door. I like to think it is the same food he is eating with his family upstairs. I wash the plates and leave them outside my door, where they are picked up by one of his children. I see them running past my basement window.

Today it is spaghetti and meatballs. I don't like noodles. I'm staring at the food and say a little prayer. Mother Anke always said we needed to be grateful for everything God gave us.

A car backfires.

I need to pack my things. They will be coming for me soon. They will take me away from my home . . .

❋

Today Mother Anke adds a few more things to her travelling trunk. She uses her whole body to push it down the hallway, closer to the front door, before walking down our front steps to sit in her wicker chair by the well. I'm not certain what she is waiting for, but I know she wants to leave and she will remain in that place until she is taken away. She does not speak. I ask her questions, but she does not respond. She wears a straw hat, its wide brim protecting her face and shoulders from the scorching sun. The tsetse flies land on her skin and bite her and she does not flick them away.

I climb up to sit on my branch in the old acacia in the clearing. From here I can watch Mother Anke through the mesh of leaves, and I can also scan the bush and the dirt road that rises over the hill. Papa does not leave on his horse anymore. Instead, he locks himself in his office and closes the shutters.

It is late afternoon in October, just before the long rains begin to fall, and the ground is scorched. The riverbed is dry, not even a trickle.

I look up across the mission. The sounds and movements around me have stopped. The jungle has become suddenly quiet. Mother Anke sits up in her chair and straightens her back, as if she has picked up the scent of something approaching. I hear a rustle in the trees. Twigs snap. Then I hear a rifle's unmistakable *cachink*. Dark shapes of a man—and then another, and another—slowly emerge from the shadow into the clearing. Behind them, a machete slashes the brush and another man steps from the trees. I look around and count seven men in military uniforms. They do not see me up in my perch.

"We came for a visit," the first man says to Mother Anke. His machine gun is slung behind his back. "We came to find God in your mission."

I allow myself a tiny breath of hope, but I am thirteen now and I can tell when men are playing. One of the men, a small man, throws his head back and laughs loudly. This annoys the first man, the toothless leader who simply holds his hand up and the small one stops. I follow the other men, who have shifted and now circle us in the clearing. Some of them are squatting and have lit cigarettes. Their machetes lie on the ground, but their guns rest across their thighs.

Mother Anke stands and pushes her straw hat off her head. It falls to her back, its string cutting across her neck. The first soldier offers his canteen to her.

"I have water," she says in Portuguese, pointing to the well. I have not heard her speak in over three weeks and I no longer recognize the tone in her voice.

"If you're going to insult me by not drinking my water, then

I should offer it to the boy in the tree," he says, turning to look straight at me.

His face is round, with large ears that stick out. His eyes are big and set far apart. Mother Anke looks up at me in the tree. I slide down. One of the soldiers has removed his boot and is massaging his sockless foot. He looks younger than the rest, a boy like me.

"My friends call me Macaco," the leader says, jiggling the canteen in front of me. I'm not certain what to do. My knees feel weak. I reach for the canteen and take a drink.

Papa Gilberto appears at the front door. The men look at him. He is not fully dressed; his suspenders lie slack by his sides, and his linen shirt is not fully buttoned to the collar. For a moment I believe Papa has been expecting these men, that he called on them to help deliver Mother Anke's trunk to the city.

"You have come to our mission and so we welcome you. Is there anything we can do for you?"

I know Papa's voice and there is no conviction in the offer.

"I think we have everything we're looking for," Macaco replies.

Papa comes down the steps to stand behind Mother Anke. He places a hand on her shoulder and attempts to direct her back into her chair. She refuses to sit. The other soldiers have begun walking from building to building with their guns raised.

"Stop!" Macaco shouts. I am ten feet away from being beside my parents. "You, boy, bring her chair here, under the branch."

I brush my father's arm and Papa whispers, "Do as you're told." I grab the back of Mother Anke's chair and drag it in the dust, making clear lines with the back legs.

"Pick it up!" the man says, and I do. I carry the wicker chair by its armrests and place it under the branch, in the spot where Lázaro used to sit.

"Now come here."

I look to Papa, who is trying very hard to keep his feet rooted to the ground.

"Animals!" Mother Anke yells.

Macaco shrugs. "What do you have hidden there?" he asks me.

I reach back and feel my slingshot tucked in my back pocket.

"Give it here," Macaco says, wiggling his finger, his palm up.

My hand shakes as my mind runs with the idea that I am quick enough to whip the slingshot from my pants, nestle a stone in its sling, and aim between Macaco's eyes. He will fall like the giant in the Bible. But Papa's face urges me to do as I have been instructed.

Macaco holds the gift Lázaro had carved for me, the only thing left of my old friend. He flings it away. "Armando, come here!" The boy uncoils rope before he approaches. "Give me your gun," Macaco tells Armando. Armando lifts the strap of the machine gun over his head and gives it to Macaco. "If you are going to be a soldier, you must use a man's weapon. Not a child's toy." Macaco presses the gun against my chest. "Take it!" he says. I clutch the wooden handle and allow my fingers to trace over the black metal of the gun's forearm and barrel. It feels strangely warm and heavy.

My back explodes with heat. The prayer house is ablaze. The other men light torches they have made and begin to touch the straw roofs of each structure on our mission. The goats run to the fields and the chickens cluck nervously, small bursts of flight to hide away from the flames. I see Papa's books being thrown out the window. His office chair is next. I look to Papa for an answer and suddenly hear the music from one of his records cutting through the roar and whistle of fire. His face shows no emotion and I am angry with him. He needs to do something before it is all gone.

"You are worse than animals!" Mother Anke holds on to the sides of her skirt.

She steps forward. Macaco does not move. Mother Anke raises her hand to smack him. He catches her swing in mid-air, holds on. "Such a fine hand," he says, lowers it to his lips and kisses it. I take a short breath. Macaco swings his machine gun and strikes the side of her head with the thick butt. Mother Anke staggers back and Papa can do nothing to soften her fall. Pee warms my inner thigh.

The boy stares at me, or perhaps at his gun. I'm not sure.

Mother Anke's eyes begin to flutter and I wish they would remain closed so she does not have to see our world burning down. But it is Papa who frightens me most. I have never seen Papa without an answer.

I want to raise the gun and fire. But I don't know how it works.

"You," Macaco says, waving his gun, directing Papa to move. "Go sit in the chair there."

Papa walks slowly to the wicker chair, his hands turned up to heaven as if he is reciting a prayer. "Go sit with your mother," he says as he brushes past me.

"Gilberto," Mother Anke says. She wobbles a bit as she stands.

Unable to let go of the gun, I walk toward Mother Anke. A trickle of blood from her temple runs down to the corner of her mouth. She is about to take a step forward to meet me but two of the men grab her and hold her arms back. Her whole body tilts forward, a final thrust to rush for Papa, who sits down in the wicker chair. The men bend Mother Anke over the well's dark opening. They pin down her arms and she holds on to the stone sides, her knuckles white with the strain. I turn back to Papa. Armando is securing him to the back of the chair with rope. In my shame, I can only look at the tips of his toes. When I do look up, his face is turned up to the sky. He is looking up at something only he can see. The smoke billows above.

The world is erased—sound, colour, movement. I am stuck in place, immovable. I do not turn from my father. I want Papa to say something, to give me a sign. I cannot stop my lips from trembling. All the air in Mother Anke has been released, poured out into the well, her body landing with a thud. Her scream echoes across the grounds.

I open my mouth.

Our mission is engulfed in flames. The searing red and orange eats away at everything I have ever known.

My eyes burn.

Macaco tells me what I must do. He helps me position the stock against my cheek. My heart knocks against my chest and the aching makes the whole world spin. Ants are crawling up my legs and the heat from the fire is sharp. I hold the gun. I feel the metal of the trigger cold against my fingertip. I feel the muzzle of Macaco's gun press at my temple. Bright stars explode in front of me.

Pó

After Fatima took her last breath, Machinga and Vasco left for the flat lands. It would take them days.

Ezequiel and I were alone at the top of the mountain. I awoke one morning feeling strong and well. I could see my future laid out in front of me like a clear path. We would start a new life far away from the men who chased after Zeca and infected his mind. I felt free making my way down the side of the mountain. I knew every inch of cliff and rock and shrub. I bathed under the waterfall and I waited for Ezequiel there.

I plunged into the pool and swam to the bottom, the water swirling around my legs and thighs, my breasts and neck. I shot up to the surface to take in a greedy gulp of air. I dove down once again, slicing through reeds at the bottom. I did not hear the distant whirr of helicopters, the rush of soldiers cutting through jungle to climb the mountain.

I wound my way up the mountain path.

In the distance I could see smoke rising from the village. Ezequiel had been gone when I left and now he'd returned, I thought. As I got closer, though, I saw that one of our huts was on fire.

"Ezequiel!" I called, running towards the flames. Between two huts a soldier appeared, followed by another. I looked behind me and saw two other men. I was trapped.

"Where is Ezequiel?" I yelled as two of the soldiers grabbed hold of my arms. I recognized one of them as the man who had been driving the car in Beira, the one who had frightened Ezequiel into silence. He lowered a stick, its tip wrapped in one of Fatima's saris. The smell of burning petrol made my mouth taste like metal. He set fire to Machinga and Vasco's hut. I tugged. The men behind me held tight.

Through a wall of smoke, another soldier emerged. He came down the path from our hut. He held a rifle. One of his legs was shorter than the other. His eyes were golden.

"Do you know who I am?" he said, before coughing into a handkerchief. He opened his hand and revealed Ezequiel's harmonica. "We saw Zeca in Beira . . . we asked around. The optometrist, the landlord of the Grande Hotel, a man by the name of Fulvio. Which led us to Padre Theuns, a most disagreeable man of God." He studied me. "What is your name?" His breath smelled like a dead animal was living inside his gut.

I would not give him my name and I would not look down at the ground. I locked him in a gaze. Shamed him.

He brought the back of his hand to my face, dragged his knuckle across my cheek. "So pale. So beautifully white," he said. "Are you a woman or are you a ghost?"

I pressed my lips tight and stared into his lion eyes. I wanted to take a bite out of the man standing in front of me.

"Perhaps we can help each other," he said, pressing the length of his rifle's barrel across my neck. The other soldiers held my arms by my side.

I struggled to stay up. My legs were beginning to buckle.

The soldiers dragged me across the clearing and held me down against the grinding stone. My body seized up. I was unable to move, unable to resist, unable to cry out. No sound, except for the faint notes of Abák's lullaby, the song I hummed over and over, the words growing clearer, my voice growing louder.

"Turn around!" I heard the man say. The men pinned me down before looking away. The man's weight pressed down on me.

The sun tried to break through the dark clouds. I saw the vultures circling the sky. My body shifted in the air and I looked down at the woman who remained in my body, held down against the grinding stone. I sang my song and let the breezes caress my skin. The lion man rammed himself against me, going through his motions, grunting like an animal.

From high above, I looked beyond the clearing down the side of Mount Gorongosa. I scanned the shimmering leaves and felt cold. My vision clear, I saw Ezequiel stumbling as he ran down the mountain's side. It looked as if he were running across the treetops. "Run, Ezequiel!" I was falling out of the sky, slipping back into my flesh and bone.

"Look away," the man grunted in my ear, pressing down harder, urging himself on. I refused to look away. I wanted him to look at me, to see me and to recognize his own impotence.

The man dug his face into my neck. His lips parted like a rabid dog's.

"You are a coward."

He cocked his arm back and punched my stomach. One. Two. Three. With the fourth brutal blow, I felt something tear away from me. I arched my back with the knifing pain.

The man stood back. The other men appeared frightened by what they heard and saw. They backed away from me as a pool of blood puddled beneath me.

Ezequiel

"I have a proverb for you." Papa Gilberto looks up through the crown of the acacia. He sees me sitting on my branch, dressed in my birthday clothing. I am thirteen today. "Are you ready?"

I nod.

But then I am a boy wandering the deserted village, the sound of cicadas drilling away at my brain . . .

Pó drops to the ground and the soldiers close in around her.

The men laugh, but they have not hurt her. It is me they want. I know I must give myself up to save Pó. As suddenly as this decision is settled, I am uncertain. The Commander has never once shown mercy. If I walk into the clearing and demand they let go of Pó in exchange for my surrender, I know he will kill us both.

Papa Gilberto looks up to the empty sky. Macaco presses his gun to my head. I see Father's big eyes—*forgive me, Father.* The bullet strikes.

I run.

My bed is soaked. I grab at the sides of my mattress until my knuckles turn white. I feel pinned down by an animal fear as the world shifts. The grinding of metal comes at me.

My bedroom door is closed. The room is dark.

I need my medication.

I hear voices. I can see him by my door. He is waiting for me . . .

❋

"Are we leaving here?" I ask, bursting the yolk with the crust of my bread.

"Filho, listen to me," he says, clucking his tongue. He scrapes his dinner into a small bowl. "There are no answers hidden here. The flock has left the mission, and it is time to rebuild. Now that you are thirteen I must speak to you as a man." He nods, urging me to agree. I nod. "I've always told you to place one foot in front of the other. One step turns to ten, then a hundred become ten thousand, and you'll always get to where you have to be. So I'm asking you now, you must look after your mother, do you hear me? I will remain behind to spread the word and rebuild the mission. Not here. I'll move to the capital, where things are safer."

"I don't want to leave you, Papa."

Papa Gilberto takes hold of my shoulders and presses down. His eyes are dark, his skin like worn leather. He breathes through his nose and I smell sour fruit.

"Listen to me. I have made arrangements for you and your mother." He kneels down by my chair and presses down my upturned shirt collar. "You'll leave next week by ship for the capital, and from there you will make your way to your mother's family in the Netherlands."

"But this is my home." I brush his hand away. I smooth my own collar into place.

"This was our home, but you must not fight me. One step will turn to a hundred and more, remember? Never look back. When I have found a new place for us, I will send for you. I will find us the most beautiful place, filho, you'll see. We will return to where it all began."

I catch the fear in Papa's eyes as he cups my ears, his palm so warm. He kisses my forehead.

"You will do as I say," he says, wedging my hand in his and pulling me out of my chair. I let him walk me out of the kitchen and down the hallway.

"I'm sorry, Papa."

His free hand rests on the door handle to his office. It stays there for a few seconds. It is enough time for me to place my hand over his. My fingers nestle between the valleys of his knuckles. I hope he invites me in, and I can lie down on the rug where we will listen to our favourite song and I can write my stories and draw pictures in my book. He'll let me crouch in the corner to apply polish to his boots and I'll buff them so fast that I'll see my face reflected on their surface. He'll drink his port and perhaps let me take a sip from his glass, and if he sees me suck my lips from its sweetness he'll pour me my own small amount in a shot glass and we will not tell Mother Anke. We'll spend the whole night this way and only when the animals go to sleep, the occasional yawn from a monkey or the grunt of a wild pig, will he help me to my bed where I will dream of skipping atop the canopy of trees.

"It's time to go to bed," he says, his voice unsteady. My hand slips from his. He steps into his office and closes the door behind him.

❋

I hold on to the bedroom doorknob to steady myself. I am cold. Papa isn't here. I open the door.

The basement is dark. A plate is set on the kitchen table. I shuffle over, my slippers tripping on a small rug. I grab on to the back of the couch to regain my balance and make my way to the food. A veil of flies lifts off the canned sardines lined on the plate.

I swallow my pill, sit back in my chair and turn the radio on. Music fills the room. I don't recognize the song. I am twenty-three and barefoot as I climb the stairs to an airplane.

A snowdrift almost covers the basement window. Hidden this way, I feel safe. A gust shifts the snow, creeping higher up. It is the colour of Pó's skin—her back—pressed against the glass.

Serafim

MY ROOM IS LITTERED with crumpled balls of paper. Page after page of impotent introductions to an article I need to submit by the end of next week.

I light my last cigarette, toss the pack onto the paper-strewn floor. The air conditioner is broken. I order up chunks of ice to my room. They melt in half an hour. I've taken to dipping my facecloth in the cold water and rolling it over my neck and shoulders.

Taking a long drag, I write, *Pó was born with albinism, a recessive trait she inherited from her dark-skinned parents. Her skin is bone white, her hair a pale orange shorn close to her head, her eyesight weak.*

It's fuckin' terrible. Earlier attempts sucked people in with pity. I have to figure this out.

I will not be returning to Brazil. My plane leaves from Beira to Maputo. From there I'm off to Cape Town to begin my new assignment—an investigative piece on worker exploitation in South Africa's wine-producing area.

Thousands of kilometres separate me from my previous life, if it could be called a life. Distance is simply measured, but time . . . time grabs ahold of your throat and doesn't let go.

Under a pale, unimpressive sky, a doctor working with albinos, or PWAs (persons with albinism), explains how misinformation about these people abounds. Locals believe they are ghosts or spirits that cannot be killed. Others believe the birth of an albino child is a curse.

Where am I going with this? Do I open with shock—inform readers that healers entice people to hack off albinos' limbs to put in magic potions that promise prosperity and cures for what ails them? Or just lay it out there: *An albino "set"—ears, tongue, nose, genitals, all four limbs—can sell for as much as $75,000?*

It's what I came to do, lay the facts bare. But that feels like a betrayal.

I switch the lights off. I remove the cap from my eighth or ninth bottle of beer, I'm not sure. The moon's light spills into my room, a long rectangular strip across the floor.

I am under no illusion about why writing this piece is so important to me. I have shed the guilt that I am using Pó's life to provide meaning to my own. I am writing it for me. It's all I have.

"What is it you want from me?" I ask out loud, and like a match striking its strip, I think I have an answer. The recordings and the transcripts I have made of Pó are an intimate invitation to experience this world through her recollections. Unencumbered. Raw. The question *What for?* comes back at me.

I flick my cigarette over the balcony, orange ember spinning.

I don't know how this story will end. But I know how it began.

I press my pencil to paper, write *They are called children of the moon.*

Pó

OPHELIA SNUCK OUT from the hotel in her pink tracksuit three days ago and has not been seen since.

Early this morning the women did not sweep or wash their clothes in the dirty water in the deep end of the pool. The men failed to gather and smoke cigarettes while playing cards or tending their tiny gardens. I did not wake up to the smell of burning coal in the hallways or the echo of children running along the corridors. Whenever one of the residents of the Grande Hotel goes missing all the squatters at the hotel go into hiding. They bar themselves in for two or three days. I understand their fear because I share it. It is a disease. Contagious.

Amalia enters and runs into my arms. Her worries are deadened in my shuka.

"Ophelia has not returned," she says.

"I will go find her, filha." I reassure Amalia with words.

I will not wait until the morning. I will go to the police station now and ask about Ophelia's whereabouts. They must be aware a child has gone missing. I never enjoy these visits. I struggle with the first steps. For two days, I have kept to my bed. There is not much more to give. But I must go. They will hold their breath when I enter the station, afraid they will breathe in my spirit. I use their fear to push my demands. Missing people often go unreported. The police ignore them. They will discuss things amongst themselves but they will not look at me.

Night seeps into the room while Amalia tinkers with the broken record player. She wants to get outside again, but I ask her to stay close by. Sitting by my lantern, she bites her tongue in concentration. It appears in the corner of her mouth, swollen, as she fiddles with screws and springs. A week ago, she dismantled the back of the box and is fitting the pieces back together. She is relentless. It will serve her well.

I miss Serafim's company. He jotted down his last scribble and left, walked away with my story.

There is a flash to the left of the hotel. It is not lightning. I catch the flare falling down. The sparkle of the tail reminds me of a shooting star. A couple of gunshots and faint cries from revellers. Often nights are filled with city noises, festivals and street parties that have been repeated for hundreds of years. No one knows when they began or why. No one cares.

The voices move along the shore, rising and fading as the wind changes direction. Honking car horns fill the night, and beams of light scan the beach and the shore before shooting up into the dark sky.

"Stay here, Amalia. Do not leave."

I place a blanket over my shoulders and slip into my boots. Amalia continues to busy herself with the record player.

In the hallway, I hear the sounds of hotel life. I pick up a child's wail seeping under a door. To my right, a man shouts obscenities. Using the walls for balance, I step carefully down the staircase. It is dark but I make my way through the entrance and into the hotel grounds. I exhale.

It has been months since I set foot among the small patches of garden and the busted concrete that once surrounded the pool. I look around. I raise my shuka to cover my head and part of my face.

The police station is an ugly place. Stagnant smells of sweat, cigarettes, and old paper have seeped into these walls and stained them the colour of a smoker's fingers. A ceiling fan cools the area above the front counter.

"I want to file a report," I say, while trying to catch my breath.

Three men are laughing over something on one of their cellphones. Their shirts cling to their backs.

I rap my knuckles on the counter. There is no need to say anything more. They all look up and then look away. It is clear from their hushed discussion that they are figuring out who will have the unpleasant task of dealing with a *branca*.

A young officer, traced circles under his armpits, approaches. The other two take their chairs behind their desks, pretending they are busy with official work.

"What is it?"

"A girl has gone missing. I'd like to report—"

"Girls go missing all the time. You should keep better watch over them, Senhora."

I let the shuka slip down to my shoulders.

The officer looks back for support, a desperate hope, I think, for someone to intercede and dispatch me.

I will not be sent away so easily. Their eyes avoid mine.

"Her name is Ophelia. She is fifteen and—"

"Girls at that age are like cats in heat." The young officer is amused with himself. When he does not hear his fellow officers chime in, his cheek begins to twitch. "Go home. She'll return soon." The officer looks down at some paperwork, then at his wristwatch. He does not look at me. Drops of sweat sit on his brow. He mops his face with a handkerchief he keeps tucked in his fist.

"You must look for her."

"And where should we begin looking? The music festival does not end until morning and the streets are crowded with people."

"What interests me is finding Ophelia," I say, but it's a struggle to finish the sentence.

"Come back tomorrow. Your daughter is probably in the arms of a young man, finding some relief—"

"I will not move from this place."

"Well then, you can stand there all night because—"

"Ramlosa!" A deep voice fills the room. A strapping man I did not see sitting behind a computer screen stands. He approaches the counter. "I am Magassela, the new captain here. This is my precinct and I'd like to apologize for the constable. There is a lot the young must still learn. Now, when did you last see the young woman? Can you describe her to me?"

"She is like me," I say, my voice unsteady.

Captain Magassela lowers his hand over my fist and squeezes. "We will find her."

I find the strength to turn away and walk out the door. I hear Captain Magassela offering me a ride home, but I am overwhelmed by his concern and don't dare take more than he has already offered. The streets are crowded with revellers. I sit outside the police station to gather my strength and catch my breath. I have not covered my head and face.

The roads are scarred with potholes. Halfway home, I take an uneven step into a divot and stumble. My knees and the heels of my palms burn, scraped red and embedded with gravel and dirt.

I cannot get up. I drag myself over to sit at the curb. One of my boots lies on its side where I fell.

A young girl of six or seven, half-naked in underwear, picks up my boot. She walks over to me and drops it within my reach. I have nothing to offer her in thanks. She swings from side to side, biting her thumbnail.

I unlace my other boot, slip it off my foot, and raise it to her. This beautiful child sits beside me and slips on both of my boots. She dances on the spot, gets a feel for their weight. Then she tries to run and trips. She does it again, and I cannot help but smile. *May the children greet her knees. May she grow to be lucky. Be oretiti tree with the spread-out roots.* I give voice to the words, sing them out loud. I get up and try to walk again. I fall twice more. I rest awhile before digging deep, finding the strength to stand and continue my way back.

When I reach the grounds of the Grande Hotel, the pulsing red light of the Coca-Cola machine hisses. I do not have the strength to climb the stairs to my room. I sit on the steps leading down to the pool to catch my breath. Aunt Simu used to say the dark sky speaks to those who look and listen to it.

I long to feel the concrete pressing against the soles of my feet.

I hear the rumble in the night air, the flash of lightning. The first drops begin. My eyes travel up towards the crumbling balconies. I see no one. Never have I felt so alone. A sharp pain cuts across my chest. My breath is gone.

Remember your name. I hear the faint words of a spirit and know it is Fatima. *Lie here by me,* the voice says, and I can smell cinnamon and clove.

"Pó," I whisper. I spread my fingers over my knees, open my mouth to drink the rain that is now falling heavily.

Remember your name.

"Simu? Is that you?" I say out loud, as a thousand thorns of rain prick at my skin. The fat drops make holes in the dust. The mud splashes on my feet. The rust-stained water begins to drain into the pool. I can smell the wet clay of Simu's skin, hear the tinkling of her jewellery in the breeze. "I have missed you, Simu."

What is your name, child?

"You named me Liloe. You said I was never to call out the name I was given at birth until I was ready to be taken back to the place I came from."

You have your power. Follow the river.

"Where are you, Simu?" I whisper, tears rising.

I look up at the hotel. All the shattered windows, the bushes that grow from cracks in its walls. Amalia inside. She is young, and there is still so much to teach her.

Call out your name. I hear the voice of my mother. I mourned the child that had lived inside me. But he survived in my mind, bright-eyed, his arms reaching out to me. We could have known such joy.

My mother's heartbeat has come back for me—grown strong and loud just as mine falters. Dried grass, earth, smoke, her polished skin, the drip-drip of rain . . . *You are my child, mine to me.*

My head grows heavy. My shuka is soaked to my skin. My body will not stop shaking. The place I came from will be covered with darkness.

"Kibo," I whisper.

The rain is coming down in sheets and the ground drinks hungrily. What it cannot take spills into the pool. Staring up at one square of yellow, my third-floor balcony, I spot Amalia in her white linen shuka. With the heavy rain and from this distance I cannot see clearly, but it looks like she is wearing my beaded collar. She holds a lantern over her head. She has fixed my soldier's music box.

The lament raises a lump in my throat. Together, the spirits call out to me. Ezequiel's song lifts and soars above the hotel.

Your name. What is your name, precious child of mine?

I want to smile. Amalia needs to know that everything will be fine. My beautiful child, slim and long-limbed, her skin the colour of night. Some residents appear at their windows and balconies. They are drawn by the unexpected song.

Your name, child?

Amalia will grow strong, good, and true. The story will continue in her. I do not know how to say goodbye. The rain comes down. I press the back of my head on the rim of the pool and look up. It is time to let the darkness cover me.

"Kibo."

I am no longer afraid. I repeat my name again, quiet but resolute.

"Kibo. My name is Kibo."

Acknowledgements

I am forever grateful for the encouragement and wisdom of my brilliant editor, Martha Kanya-Forstner. She knows how to make everything better. To my tireless publicist, Scott Sellers, thank you. Special thanks to Amy Black, Susan Burns, Kristin Cochrane, Zoë Maslow, Shaun Oakey, Terri Nimmo and Ward Hawkes. A special thanks to Paige Sisley. I also owe much to my incredible agent, Dean Cooke.

This book would not be in your hands if it were not for my trusted early readers. I want to thank them for their friendship and support: Susan Mockler, the late Bernie Grzyb, James Papoutsis, Rekha Lakra, Susan Shuter, Sheila Murray, and Hendrika Haasen.

I would like to thank my uncles and the many veterans I interviewed who relived their experiences with me. A special thanks to Gilberto Do Rego Sousa and his wife, Connie Almeida Sousa.

I am indebted to the staff of both the Canadian and Tanzanian branches of Under the Same Sun, an NGO committed to supporting and educating people with albinism in Tanzania. Special thanks to Peter Ash, founder and CEO of UTSS, for agreeing to have me shadow him on a visit to Tanzania. I want to thank Don Sawatzky for keeping me informed. Special thanks to Vicky Ntetema, a remarkable woman who works tirelessly to educate and protect the human rights of people with albinism. To all the unforgettable people, many of them children, who shared their stories of living with albinism. To find out more, including how you can help people with albinism, please visit www.underthesamesun.com

Deep gratitude to Gregory Carr, an American entrepreneur and philanthropist committed to the restoration of Mozambique's Gorongosa National Park. Working alongside him is the passionate Vasco Galante, Director of Communications. What they shared with me became essential to the writing of this book. A special thanks to everyone who made my visit to Gorongosa unforgettable: Barbara Matadinho, Leonardo Mandevo, Moutinho Nhongo, and Yannik Bindert. To learn more about the important work these individuals do, please visit http://www.gorongosa.org. In Beira, a special thanks to

Graem White and Carrie Davies. I am also grateful to Mário Pinto, who did the unthinkable and managed to secure access to the Grande Hotel to walk its halls and meet with many of its residents.

And finally, as ever, thanks and love to my sons, Julian, Oliver, Simon, who always make me want to do better, be better. And to my wife, Stephanie, to whose love this book is dedicated.

A NOTE ABOUT THE TYPE

Children of the Moon has been set in Scala, a type family created in the late 1980s by Martin Majoor, a book typographer and type designer based in The Netherlands. The principle forms of Scala are derived from humanist faces such as Bembo and Fournier, yet feature lower contrasts and stronger serifs—ideal for modern electronic book design and typesetting. Of particular note is the rare balance and compatibility of the serif and sans serif. Originally designed to address the peculiar challenges of setting multiple levels and weights of information within a music concert programme, Scala is named after the Teatro alla Scala in Milan.